THE VOYAGES OF
ALFRED WALLIS

THE
VOYAGES OF
ALFRED WALLIS

Peter Everett

JONATHAN CAPE
LONDON

Published by Jonathan Cape 1999

2 4 6 8 10 9 7 5 3 1

First published in Great Britain by Jonathan Cape 1999

Jonathan Cape
Random House, 20 Vauxhall Bridge Road,
London SW1V 2SA

Random House Australia (Pty) Limited
20 Alfred Street, Milsons Point, Sydney,
New South Wales 2061, Australia

Random House New Zealand Limited
18 Poland Road, Glenfield,
Auckland 10, New Zealand

Random House South Africa (Pty) Limited
Endulini, 5A Jubilee Road, Parktown 2193, South Africa

Random House UK Limited Reg. No. 954009

Extract from 'Lines on Roger Hilton's Watch'
Copyright Estate of W. S. Graham

A CIP catalogue record for this book
is available from the British Library

ISBN 0-224-05987-4

Papers used by Random House UK Limited are natural,
recyclable products made from wood grown in sustainable forests.
The manufacturing processes conform to the environmental
regulations of the country of origin

Typeset by Deltatype Limited, Birkenhead, Merseyside

Printed and bound in Great Britain by
Creative Print and Design (Wales), Ebbw Vale

To SVEN BERLIN – for his book on Alfred Wallis, without which I could not have written this fiction

When I woke up this morning I was on top of Susan. The voices in the chimney were scolding – not that I could make out what they said. If I hear them when I'm about that business, I take fright. I never know what they might want me to do. Mrs Peters had come knocking at the window to see how I was, and I told her that King Herod used to lie with his wife after she died. She said that was not fit for a Christian woman to hear, first thing in the morning.

Susan knew more than I did, being a widow. I was asleep, and the next thing I feel her creep into my bed. What to do for the best? I lie still, saying nothing. All I can think is, I'm never going to manage, but I didn't have to. She pulls up her nightdress, and then I feel her hand come sliding round. She has me stiff before I know; her breath roars in my ear, a rise and fall; I gape as fish do, spurting into her hand. She is moaning now. She pulls me round and takes my hand between her thighs. She slips a thimble on my finger and makes me to rub it where she wants, or drive it up inside her. Her moaning now will wake the house. A sin in the mind is out there before you can deny it. Next thing you know, it's in the flesh and you revel in it while it lasts.

When it's over, she leans across to give my forehead a kiss, and goes back to her bed. Next morning, I hear her singing a hymn, and the thimble is back in her workbox on the sideboard, where it belongs. Nothing is said about it. Things go on as usual. Then, a week later, she comes again with a better idea of what she wants. She has thighs like a hurdler when she sits astride me, saying, 'If you want this so much, I think that you and I better get wed.'

She was very sparing of herself after we did. I felt she would only do it because she had her heart set on twenty babies to get a letter from Buckingham Palace.

Women are deep, far deeper than any man is. We are Mayflies skating on a pond, and that's how they leave us when they go. Her first husband, Jacob Ward, used to be a garden labourer in Madron. She had seventeen children by him when he died. She was forty-two, a lace worker who had made a cap for Queen Victoria's child. She sold her work to Mr Blamely after she came to live in Penzance.

I met her through her son, George, who was a good friend. He was a waiter at the Penzance Hotel when I first went with him to New Street. Susan took me in as a lodger. I could hear her skirts as she went about the room, then before I could say a word she knelt in front of me with a cloth and began to rub at a stain on my trousers. 'You better change your messy ways if you live here,' she said, pressing my leg. It was left like that: I could take it how I wanted. I was blushing up to the roots of my hair, and sweat broke out across my back and round my shirt collar.

George used to be the first person I'd seek out, soon as my ship lay at berth. All that my shipmates were raring to get ashore for was drink and fornication: 'We're dry as dirt,' they'd say. 'Come along of us down the pub, Alf, and wet your whistle.' I would never go; I was teetotal. Only time I ever drank spirits was when I was given up for dead aboard ship, so cold I couldn't lift my arms. One thing, though – I can never do without my baccy.

Captain Roach awoke, as any captain would, when heavy seas hit his ship. We all did. Some waves come with such force and weight that they can break a deck like an eggshell. You hear that, and you know why the mate is at the fo'c'sle door. You run out and you are in the sea, and more of it is coming over the side. You don't walk; the wave hurls you along the deck, where the second mate is hanging on and screaming at you to get aloft. The lightning gives you half a glimmer of the list as you go down and hit the rail. Others are already climbing to furl what is left of the sails. We are to ride out the gale hove-to.

Not one of those sails is in one piece; most are rent, while others have blown clean away in the dark. She lies for hours with big seas over her rails.

At dawn, the bos'n shakes us up to fix what was torn and lost. No sooner do we do so than she springs a dire leak. All hands set to work on the bilges. We are only able to get inshore because the captain knows an old dodge, and has us cast a sail under the bow. We toss down any waste bit of wood, wool and rope, so that they suck into the hole.

I make mugs of beef tea against the cold. Unless we keep on at the chain-pumps, we will founder. You hate those pumps; your life depends on the work, but it is fit only for convicts. Even then the sea gains on us. We are lucky to bring her inshore to shelter. There, we find out why we took on so much water: a leeward plank has rotted round its bolts, so we can see daylight. If one is like that, there are others. Unless you give the sea respect at all times, even when it's glassy calm, you are a dead man. All that stands between you and eternity is a two-inch plank.

But that was not the end of it. We patched that hole and set off again. Some bad weather seems to follow you, or lies in wait. Three squalls began to dog us, crossing one after the other astern. They break the rudder at the waterline, shearing bolts away and bending others. Are we to abandon ship? When the weather does ease, we see that the stern-post is still in one piece, but we are in need of a miracle, a calm sea to fix the rest. Soon as it does abate, we hammer those bolts that are bent, get them straight. Idling under short sail, we shape, nail, and bolt three thicknesses of plank together; then, drifting in gentler waters, fix the rough rudder in place. By now, it seems the whole ship is crank, and I am in a bad dream.

It was Christmas; I had an abcess as big as a hen's egg on my neck. I was in a seaman's boarding house in Gloucester. If you were in need of a ship, you would go to such a place. Most boarding-house keepers, or mistresses, know who has come ashore and what ship wants hands. Of course there are crimps among them, too, who will sell you to a captain for a month's pay. You can come to under some cruel master working yourself to death for nothing.

The house was a poor hole. All I had to look at, or think about, was a picture of George Washington crossing the Delaware.

I was glad to see the ladies of the Mission to Seamen when they came. They were going around those houses, and the ships in harbour, looking for sailors to feed and succour. They had a girl with them called Alice Fincher. Almost a child still, she had been living with a seaman who took ship when she got pregnant. The child died at birth, since when

4

the Mission ladies had taken her under their wing. If they had seen her flirt among the seamen as she went with tracts, they might have had second thoughts.

Alice Fincher would never mind changing my poultices when the Mission women asked her to, nor did she turn away when the abcess burst. She washed it clean with a bowl of warm salt water and bathed it over with iodine. I was glad Mr Vinnicombe had cut my hair.

Grateful, I was able to go around the streets without pain.

Ever after that, I did not know why, Miss Fincher began to follow me about. I would run into her everywhere. Even at night, white as a moth she would flit around corners where I was walking.

There was a moon; scudding clouds that laid shadows on a silver sea. I ran up to her quickly before she could go. I was afraid to face her that way, but I had to do something. Under cover of night, she would not see my blushes. I said, 'Is there anything you want, Miss Fincher? I keep seeing you.'

She said she could not say why. She felt so lost she had to walk the streets and I was always there. 'It was love. I looked to love to save me, but it didn't,' she said.

'Can't the Mission women help?'

'They took care of me, and still do; I am grateful.'

I did not ask about the sailor, any more than when I met Susan I wanted to know about Jacob. I would tell myself that she must have found something to like about him to get all those children.

Alice said she had no family, but was used to that. She was an orphan; hearing this, my heart went out to her. She had eyebrows black as tadpoles, but the loveliest thing about her was that she was small enough for me to look into her eyes. I felt that nothing I said to her was lost. Then again, nothing's plain sailing, as we say.

I asked whether she was not afraid of the night.

'I don't mind it,' she said. 'I never did. I used to search my soul at night; they still say I ought to do it, but I can find nothing. My life is better than it was, but it is not what I want. I want to live in a big city, but I'm afraid to go. I fear what could happen to me.'

I said I did not think I could live in a city.

'Are you a married sailor, Mr Wallis?'

For a sailor to marry is not fair on the poor woman, I said. She is left there ashore for months to wonder whether he's dead or alive. Letters? It's hard to find any time to spend on yourself, to wash your clothes, darn holes or even grease your sea boots.

On New Year's Eve there was a dance she wanted to go to. Standing in the doorway when we got there was her friend Zoë, and I did not like her at all. She was only friendly because she envied Alice.

Her nose was big in a pale face, and her blouse was so fine you could see all the struts and braces of her underwear. She was shapeless beside Alice, even though she was younger – seventeen years old, I guessed – but there were blue shadows under her eyes. I felt better when she had her coat on, or was warmly dressed. She was not happy with her lot, and you could hear it in her sighing and see it in the sullen look she had. Alice said she was pining for a boy called Burt, who had let her down over the dance. She would improve later, I'd see, if she could let herself go. It was true. She went around like a whirlwind on the floor, never minding who she bumped into.

The ceiling of the hall was too low, and the air was full of smoke, perfume and sweat. Never mind that all the windows were open, the men had their ties undone and the women, all hot and flustered, fanned their cheeks. Alice got me out on the floor to waltz. I couldn't do the steps but she put one of my hands on her little bottom as she shook it from side to side, saying, 'Give me a tight hug, why don't you. You know it's what you want to do.'

When I had to piss, I could not find the head and went outside. I could hear the chickens in the dark; then I began to make them out, going to and fro behind the wire. A door opened, and a woman stood in the light with a bowl of corn to feed them. I hoped she could not see where I was in the shadow.

Alice always wore her glad rags, a blue dress, hat and gloves; so I had to try to be a dandy in my Sunday best shore-going suit.

'Don't be shy, Alfred,' she would say.

I did my best to obey her; though I could not help but think of the time when I would have to go. I would see her standing on the wharf to wave, and that would be hard to bear.

Some days went by, and I did not see Alice. There was no sign of her. She had gone. I went to the canning factory where Zoë worked to ask her if she knew anything. It was hot in there, a terrible din going on. All she did was shake her head, and make out she had to get back to her place. I did not like the smell; no wonder it let her beauty down, and she was so pale. So after I got through asking at the boarding houses, I went to the ladies of the Mission. They were very cold; all they knew was that Alice Fincher had found herself another sailor. I said yes, she had, and that I was the man.

'Be glad she left, Mr Wallis,' said a Mrs Spicer. 'A girl like that is natural-born to create havoc.'

She had come to collect some things she had, saying that she was going to marry Willem, a Dutchman.

All I could find out was that he was from Arnhem, and that he had found them berths on board a vessel headed for Antwerp.

In the end, I had to think that it was as well that it turned out that way. What would I have done, stayed there? Never gone home again to the West Country?

Let's see how we stand now. I am not my own master in this matter; I want to think I am, but it isn't so.

'Get aloft, there! Reef the royals and top-gallant sails!' Those were the mate's orders. A cargo of West Indian sugar for Liverpool, wool, nitrate, or tea was fine, but I had no relish for that guano from North Peru. That's gull shit they bring up from Chincha Island to use for manure. The birds have been going there so long that the stuff lies fifty, sometimes two hundred, feet deep. They send convicts to dig it and put it in bags. They put the bags in lighters and ferry them out to the ships at anchor. A ship can lie there three months loading, and the air is yellow, everything is yellow on board.

We were waiting at Veracruz to take that cargo off a vessel that had run into bad weather. The helmsmen had had great trouble to hold her steady with heavy seas coming aft, and one was swept away when handing over the wheel. The waves battered her then, so badly she was no longer seaworthy. Their chief trouble, though, was that they had an escaped convict aboard. Hunger and the storms and the stink of that ammonia had driven him mad, and he cut two holes with an axe in her side. They thought he had been hoping to force the ship into harbour, so that he could swim ashore. I could not have stayed in that hold for an hour, let alone weeks. He came out shrieking like a dervish, wearing a hood; he had cut up one side of a sack. He was trying to get over the side when the captain shot him. 'We were lucky he

8

did not set fire to the ship,' he said. 'Throw his body over.'
As it was, she had leaks enough to be listing in the water.

How were we to get that guano aboard? We gave some
Mexicans a few pesos to do that, and then the *Hormuz* began
to stink.

We left Veracruz, blithely trying to make a joke of the
stench, for what else could we do? Soon we were miles off
course, and becalmed. People use that word: drifting. They
don't know what it means unless they have been to sea.
People have no notion what it's like to drift at the mercy of
the waves. God's is the only eye then that can see you, the
only ear to hear your cry. In Him you put your trust. There is
nothing else. Yes, at sea you must keep a close eye on
Providence.

There was no breath of wind, and the *Hormuz* lay idle, day
after day. All you could feel was that she would never move
again. The ammonia smell got worse off all that shit in the
hold in the blistering heat. Week after umpteenth week there
was no cloud, no rain, and no sign of any ship. After dark,
the air was still and close; it beat like a drum, unless what I
could feel was my heart coming up into my throat to stifle
me. All day we lay on deck under a tarpaulin, parched,
longing for the mate to dole out the fresh water, which we
knew was running out. The lower it fell in the tank, the more
brackish it tasted. Even worse, most of the food we ate was
salt. As to washing, there was only a bucket of sea water. It
would cool your face but, as the heat laid open every pore,
you soon got sores.

We'd tap the barometer for any sign of it falling, ready
with everything on deck to catch rain: old sails, tarpaulins,
longboats, buckets, even bowls. We'd stand staring at that
hard blue sky, straining our eyes for any shadow of a cloud.
There was none, day after day, until at eight bells on a

Sunday a faint wisp began to grow on the starboard bow. Not a cloud, no, it was more of a blur, but it became a cloud of sorts, the first sign of that deluge we were praying for. Long swells came running first; they set the *Hormuz* shaking under a darkening sky. We had taken down every stitch of sail; the masts were bare. If there had been any canvas up there that great onrush would have taken the sticks out of her or turned us over easy. When the gale struck, it came on the starboard bow and ran down her side, heeling her over with the weight of tons of water. Seeing it come, we had tied ourselves to masts and rails. We did not look; we knew that those waves were fifty feet high. When the clouds burst we ran naked in the pelting rain, dancing like savages – all except Mr Vinnicombe, who had been low and in a bad way all through the business. Any niggling doubt or fear became harder to bear by the hour. Days would pass and that fear grew worse in your head. It would seep into every bone, your liver, your spleen, and spread with every breath you took. That brassy weather made us all do freak things – even the fish were mad, more so than Mr Vinnicombe. I could only think that the tops of the mountains under the sea had burst off, and set going fast whirlpools in the deep that brought up the fish that live there, with their innards blown out of their mouths.

After the rain, a wind rose of such fury that we had to get up in a rush, and we were naked as we set the sails. When they were up, she ran before that gale for twenty-five or thirty miles, until it died away and left us idling again.

There was more of the same, except we had water now. Most of us felt better, except Mr Vinnicombe. He was an old sailmaker, a Devon man who had been on whaling ships when he was younger. He used to tell how he had sailed in Samuel Enderby's ships that voyaged round the Horn to kill whales for women's corsets. All those vessels had great captains, men the Royal Navy had taught to sail.

We had made port, miles from where we should be, where the crimps had heard of the trials we had been through. One came aboard with an offer of berths on a ship bound for Liverpool. They were always ready with offers to men who had gone through a hard time. None of the crew would listen to him, but Mr Vinnicombe did go ashore with his chest in the crimp's boat. Some days later we found a letter with his mattress and bedding leaving them to Mr Ogletree. I was to have some tools he had left behind. Since he had signed his ship's articles of agreement, all of us expected him to be back in time to sail. He had always been among the first aboard. The letter knocked everything on the head. I said I would go ashore to ask that crimp if he had taken him up on his offer of a berth, to find out why he had not come and where he was.

The crimp said he had thought Mr Vinnicombe funny in the head, and had soon given up on him.

Mr Vinnicombe had called in at the agent's to ask whether he had any letters from his mother; she was so frail she was barely alive. She was on his mind a lot during our ordeal. They had given him three pounds to send her, after he begged them. The last they had seen of him he was drinking in a bar across the road.

Going there, I heard that he had been with some sharper who had got him drunk and left him short of his duffel-bag and chest. I had seen in that chest. He had it all in there: treasures. Inside the lid was a photograph of every ship he had sailed on, pictures and postcards from Yokohama and other cities in the world. He had music boxes and shells, Tarot cards, an accordion, old dresses, fans and Japanese dolls. He had a floral chamber-pot, necklaces and ivory carvings, and a turtle shell. It was all stuff he was taking home, which never seemed to get there over the years. If the police could not find those things – well, I surely could. The only stuff I've seen like it since has been in Mr Armour's shop. I think of Mr Vinnicombe every time I go in there.

To lose his chest must have struck him an awful blow. It was the police who sent me to the asylum. They had picked a man up who had been sleeping in a church and woken up screaming after a nightmare. He could not tell them his name, where he had come from, or where he was going.

I sat in a small dark garden at the asylum before I found the courage to go up the creaky wooden steps to the front door to see whether the man was Mr Vinnicombe; I knew he had never gotten over our ordeal in the doldrums.

The house was built of wood, and so ramshackle a stiff wind would blow it away. I went up stairs that led to more stairs and corridors with so many twists and turns they were full of whispers and echoes. All the windows had stained glass, but the place had nothing to do with religion. I was afraid I'd never find my way out again. Ever upward I went until I found him on the top floor. There, I could almost touch the ceiling. The room was cold, so I guessed they had decided that he was an incurable. The nurse said that in a whisper – it was not worth trying to do anything for most of them. Mr Vinnicombe's eyes were open, but nothing else. He would not speak, nor did he seem to hear what I said, although I kept off anything to do with times past. I did not want to rub salt into his wounds.

They did not know what best to do for him, or how to treat him. He would not tell them his wants. So the writing was on the wall for him. He did not have a cat's chance in hell. He would die there, a long way from Devon.

Just as I had decided I was getting nowhere and was about to go, he said, 'The sun is going down.'

It was not the start to anything. It was the last thing he had on his mind.

I ran out faster than I went in.

He can strike when you least expect Him; a glancing blow will lay you low. He is always near at sea; if He is not, you never get home: any big wave can take you; a blow on the head, and you forget who you are; a cut can turn so bad you lose a limb.

The weather was clear when we cried Godspeed to our sister ship at St John. What time you leave a place can often make a difference to whether you live or die. How could we know that they would run foul of a storm the day after and all sink? The same bad weather was laying for us, too, off the Grand Banks. We were going along with studding-sails set; as she came upon the wind she would feel it the more, and we went aloft to furl the skysails. It was all a mess – we had it all to haul in, everything flying. The topmast studding-sail boom, buckling and jumping out, broke at the iron. I was clewing-in the main-top-gallant studding-sail, but the tack was shorn away, off went the shroud, whipping to and fro. I clung tight to the mast, going this way and that in the fading light, and a keen wind drove the rain hard at my face. 'Nearer my God to Thee,' I heard myself cry like a babe. The halyards were at that second let go by the run, and I had to fight a devil to get what was left of it into the top. I was making it fast when the mate cried, 'Lay aloft there! Furl that main!'

I did not want to go out on that yard. They had let go the braces, and the thing was swinging back and forth, and the sail blowing out to leeward; the lee-leech was over the yard arm, with the royal adrift and lashing over my head. I looked down; nobody could hear my shout. When a man falls off, he breaks every bone in his body. I had seen it happen. It was the helmsman who saw the plight I was in, and got help to haul on the ropes.

We were being beaten as we rolled in the troughs; the ballast had begun to shift, so that our cargo of fish was moving, too. To trim the ship, a line of men stood passing the cod along to toss them over the side, fighting to stay afoot with each wave. I lost all feeling in my hands. At first light we came to, our eyes red but alive. Bone-tired, we lay below deck, too weary to shed our oilskins that glowed with a scum of fish scales.

Before light the rain came on again, and we took four days of bad weather under close sail all the time being blown off course.

Told that I was lost at sea, Susan gave birth before term. It was a boy she called Alfred, but he died at two months, before I got home.

I did not mean to give up going deep-sea, but after that voyage I stayed too many days ashore and Susan went on so. I had bad trips many a time, but after that fright I told myself I had made up my mind. So I started fishing out of Mousehole and Newlyn aboard the *Flying Scud*. The farthest I went after that was Scotland.

Susan was with child again. The boy I knew nothing about until it was over, but I was there when Ellen Jane died of convulsions.

Nothing is more hurtful than to hear a baby cry for pain; it lets go a burst of wails, then has to sob to get its breath, sobs that wrack its body something awful. I was glad when the Lord in His mercy saw fit to take her. Some nights then I lay awake; I could not sleep at all. There was nowhere to go except to walk the streets, to go down by the sea. There, I felt calmer.

My brother Charles had married and was in the marine rag-and-bone line. He would buy old fishing boats, do them up and sell them on. He could have been well off, but he drank his profits away and let things go. He sold his stuff to Mr Denley, who was shrewder, a man who wore the same old suit week in, week out and never cut his hair. He would never spruce up, even on a Sunday. A tight man with cash, he was as short as I am, but richer. You could always see Mr Denley's place when the sun shone on the brass helmet of the torn diving suit he had hanging up.

I met him one morning at the Trinity House store in Penzance. He was there to look at some buoys they wanted rid of, he said. He asked me why there were so many kinds, and I told him the names: spheres, cans and cones. I said they used them to mark different shoals. 'You know a lot more than Charlie does about marine scrap,' he said. 'You ever thought of getting into the business?'

I said no, I was working for Mr Beasly or fishing out of Newlyn, and had never thought to do anything else.

'How old are you now, Mr Wallis, if you don't mind my asking?'

I gave a laugh at that. If I was going his way, I could have a ride on his pony and trap, he said. Didn't I think I had seen enough of the sea now, having to put out in all sorts of weather to fish? Life ashore would be easier, and he would wager I'd make a better living. 'If you were to go into the scrap line in St Ives,' he said, 'I'd make you a loan to get a start.'

It took the wind out of Charlie's sails. He wanted to know where he stood, for he went there often for stuff. There could not be room for two of us. Denley was up to his tricks, and I had better watch my step, for he would do me down first chance he got. Susan was happy. She was all for it; her sons were living there, see. So I hired a horse and cart from Mr Denley to bring our bed and other goods – some big iron scales – over the moor while Albert and his new wife Margaret drove the donkey cart behind. When they married, Albert was back in his work clothes before the day was out – always a one to make on. He had lived in St Ives some time. He had been with Mr Nichols of Penzance since he was fourteen, a baker up there on the corner of New Street. Now he had his own business along Wharf Road.

You know, I'm a foreigner here, same as the day we came: Alfred Wallis, Dealer in Marine Stores. You would know the place I had on Market Strand by the scrap against the wall. I had the donkey, then, that died. People called me 'Old Iron' – 'Rag-abone!' I shouted as I went about. I rang a handbell then, but I had to give it up; there were too many complaints.

Any family as wanted to move house would come to me, too, and I would do it. One family I moved was the Bohennas.

Same as a lot of fishermen, old Mr Bohenna had been deep-sea when he was younger. Some men are lucky; one or two I've known didn't come ashore until they were over seventy years old. They had been afloat the best part of forty years. He was getting on when I first come here, but he would go down to the harbour to see what he could never have again.

'You're looking at me,' he said. 'Do you know me?'

'Not to speak to, Mr Bohenna,' I said. 'I used to see you going about the town.'

'Not lately, though.'

16

'No,' I agreed. The look in his eyes was enough to make anybody nervous. I knew then what he was about, and I said to myself, if I ever got into that state I would tie a rock to my ankle and jump off the pier at high water.

'He is losing the use of his legs,' Mrs Bohenna said. 'They swell up, and his feet hurt him all the time.'

She said to him, 'How are your legs today?' And he said, glaring at me, 'Who wants to know?'

She could not tell what to do with him. He won't eat some days, she whispered. Then said aloud, 'What are we going to do with you, Mr Bohenna, eh?'

He did not look at her at all, as if to say, nobody can see me now; I'm not here. I got him up beside me on the cart with the last load and took the reins.

'You going to make a go of it down there, then, Mr Bohenna?'

'Make a go of it? Make a go? I don't see myself doing that, and the reason is – I'm buggered if I want to.'

'Is prayer any help, Mr Bohenna?' I said. 'Do you ask God for anything?'

'A quick death; come get me out of this.'

Mrs Bohenna walked down to the corner with me. She was leaning on her stick as she looked out across the harbour. 'He has got to settle now for this here,' she said. 'Is it for the best, though? Will it be worse here, more tantalizing for him? I have used up all the money we had to do it.'

I could not get that old man out of my mind. I tossed and turned and woke up in the night. Susan was still asleep. We lay side by side as we might be in one grave, except that we were both breathing lightly. Her hands were folded on her breast, at rest, very pious.

Did she never have bad dreams? I sat up to see my white

face in the mirror. In a bad dream, the eel had strangled the bird that had got it in its beak before it had time to knock it dead on a rock.

Not always, but if you're lucky, you can fill a net in thirty seconds, or you can drift for hours and not catch a sprat. Just before one Christmas, some gigs fished their nets so full of herrings they had to cut them away. There were fish casks galore in the harbour then, and the big fish laid out in rows on the Slip.

Any time the sea was rough along the Strand the waves kept us all indoors, so I was happier when we moved to Bethesda Hill. There, I had the use of four rooms up the steps above a fishing cellar. When I went in there, out of the sun, I had to blink to get used to the dark. Only flashes of light got in so you would see where the green bottles were, or a bit of cloth, some rusty iron. The looking-glass was broken. It was high up on the wall, tilted so that I thought I was standing at the bottom of a well when I was looking up at it. The cellar I used to store the scrap and stable the horse. You could smell pilchards everywhere, as well as in every other inch of court and yard in St Ives. It was worse in season; you could not breathe for them.

Late summer then, the huers sat up on the cliff on lookout for pilchard shoals in the bay. 'Heva!' they cry. 'Hevaa!' Out of the moving shadow they make, the fish leap up to fleet and play along the surface. The huers and half the town are shouting now. The huers will shake a bush this way and that to signal boats where to shoot the seine-net around the shoal. Then there was all that banging on the boats to drive the fish into the net, and after a great to-do it was tied. The huers shout a loud halloo, and the men start to haul the catch into the shallows. There, the boats of the tuck men wait, ready with a smaller net. All the town's dogs bark now. The whole of Downalong is out to see the first pilchards come thrashing up for the dippers' baskets. As the tide turns, the men could get over among the fish and use a two-man net on a pole to scoop them into the boat, which was soon full to the gunwales. Then the fish went ashore for men to shovel into carts and run them up to the salting house. The women and girls there earn threepence the day to bed the fish down on edge, layer upon layer. At the door, the lads wait for each laden cart, ready to grab what fish they can before the boy with the cane can cut their hands. It's getting dark in there; they light the lanterns to go at it some more. The air turns cold as we stand; Susan's lips go blue, yet we don't move. The women spread more salt on the floor to pack another layer.

Down goes the tuck again! Nothing to see of the fish ashore now except the points of their noses and tails stuck out of the brown salt. They lie there buried five to six weeks until their oil leeches out into wells, then they will give them a wash in salt water and fill up hogsheads that hold two thousand and more. What days!

There were shoals enough then for six lookouts. They took up a million fish in a good year to ship to Italy and Spain, Friday fish to cram priests' bellies. Huers had a guinea for a sighting and a share of the catch. Oh, Mother, I saw the last seine shot in 1924. Even in those days, you could not buy one for less than one hundred and seventy pounds.

How old were we then? Susan was fifty-eight; I was going on thirty-six. I would still fish on the *Two Sisters* and the *Faithful* sometimes. Our neighbour up in Bethesda Place was a Mrs Bryant, who would go at Susan on the steps below. Both stuck to their guns, until Susan fired a broadside, saying, 'I think we're going to get on together, you and I,' and to that forwardness Ellen Bryant said, 'You may well find yourself erring in that.' Seems when she told her husband, he thought that Susan was a woman who stood high in the sight of God. He went out fishing. He was a man I could talk to, and did. When John Wesley came to preach at St Ives he used to stay at their house up there. Mr Bryant let me look through the telescope that he had left his father. Mr Wesley was in Cornwall in 1743. He was eighty years old the last time he came, in 1789. 'Patience, Mr Wallis,' said Ellen Bryant, 'it took Mr Wesley a sight long enough to get his foot in the door.' By then, she was keeping my books and writing all the letters.

We kept a duck and chickens, too. Trouble with those was that our neighbour, Mrs Lander, had poultry. The birds would all scratch about the alley peaceful enough except for a demon rooster she had. That fowl liked nothing better than to fly over the wall to jump on my hens and try to kill my rooster. What to do? She was not a woman I wanted any truck with, so I wrote to George. He had married and gone to farm in Devon. I was threshing once when I stayed at George's place, humping bags of grain onto the cart. If we hadn't had a cider barrel to dip into, I don't know how I would have come through that afternoon. The air was stiff as starch with dust and straw flying. Now he had lost an arm and leg to a threshing machine.

I asked him to send one of those fighting cocks bred for the ring. I could see murder in its one red eye between the bars of the crate, when it came. I could hear its wings; it was mad to be out. Fierce as that bird was, though, it would eat corn out of my hand. I let it go, the next time her rooster got on the wall. Up flew mine, and with one slash of its cruel spurs it did for Lander's bird. Alleluia! It has to be said. Mr and Mrs Lander were not best pleased. I said I hoped they were satisfied with that, and sent the rooster home to George as I had promised.

Mr Denley sent a wagon over once a fortnight; each pair of horses could haul a ton. They come over the moors, on the Nancledra road.

Mr Gilbert would say, 'They're a tight lot in St Ives, but you seem to be making a go of it.'

'Enough to get by.'

'You get some fair old loads,' he said.

No matter how you dress it up, I said, there are not many pleasures in this business, but I got to do it, day in, day out. I am in the open air and in sight of the sea. I am friendly with the donkey, and he is always good company.

I would go over with him beside his cart, and then walk back with any stuff Denley did not want. It used to give Mr Gilbert a laugh to see me walk, the more so when I said the donkey had enough to do to pull the cart.

When the donkey died, I sold his poor old carcass to the fellmonger for dog meat and glue, then set off for Dartmoor to buy a pony. He was white. I called him Albert as we walked home. Cost me fourteen pounds. I used to take him on the Island to frisk around a stake on a long rope, which I did to give him freedom. I would lie there chewing a grassblade, and we got on just fine together. If I fell asleep at all, Albert would come blow his sweet grassy breath in my face.

The time she lived at Madron, Susan was a full-time chapelgoer. She and Jacob both sang in the choir there. After Jacob died and she came to Penzance, she took up with the Salvation Army. In St Ives, the Army had a loft on Market Strand next door to where I used to have my business. I was there to help clear up the mess when the barracks caught fire in the war. I found the brass tip of the banner pole that said, 'Blood and Fire'. They got a fine building there now, just by the Lifeboat House. We used to meet in cottages then, and I would pump the organ on my knee for the hymns. They made Susan a Company Guard – a Sunday-school teacher. She would wind up the gramophone and put on the Regent Hall Band playing 'Onward Christian Soldiers'.

The Salvation Army was the only thing I joined, apart from ships. Going aboard, the captain would puff a cigar and warn you about toeing the line. A captain will walk the deck, or go whenever suits him. Some you do not see at all; others are always there, an eye to everything. They would all make a speech you knew by heart before you set foot on ship, all about what they had come to expect. After that, the first mate would split the crew into port and starboard watches. He had the port watch; the second mate had starboard. I remember that first time I went on a ship, miserable and scared in the night among the spare sails, ropes and hawsers in the steerage. There was a rough sea; my mattress, goods and gear – everything was strewn all over. I was sick as a dog. I could feel how wet the fo'c'sle was, and there was a bad smell from the bilges. You lie there in a cold bunk and try to feel how snug and warm you were in bed between your sister and your brother. All that you lose is never equal to what you become after that, yet I took it in my stride, soon found my feet.

The Army comes marching along Market Strand. 'Whosoever believeth in Me shall be saved,' the Major said. Susan was one of the whosoevers, she said, quick to sing her favourite hymn, 'T' Would Ring the Bells of Heaven'. Even the gulls on the roof of the Sloop there held their squawking at the drums banging, trumpets blaring, and tambourines ajingle-jangling. It was always about sunset time; the air would hold fire still above the calm of high water, the kittiwakes bob on the swell.

You'd think because he built the pier that John Smeaton did the light, too, but Mr Harvey put it there. The old light became a store when the council made the pier longer at a cost of five thousand pounds. To get it back they put up the harbour dues. Stothert and Pitt of Bath built the new light. It was a fixed light, and they lit it in September 1890, three months after they finished work on the pier. It was all knocking down and building then. They laid a new road through Barnoon.

We had all got along to see Jacob wed Elizabeth Stevens, all except George. He was with us then at Bethesda Hill, coughing up his life with tuberculosis, so we left him at home. With that, I could not but feel a sense of gloom all through the day. He had bought her a bracelet with charms: a half moon, an elephant, a fish, a star, a dice and a sixpence.

Anything I got in my mind is set firm there, you see. I can be wrong about dates unless I write them in the Bible; other things people tell you you got to hang onto like a raft at sea because the whole damn thing will shift about so. It's all clear as day to me, what somebody looked like as he said this or that, but if you want to know where he stood or what the date was, that's another thing entirely.

There was a bad gale they named after the *Cintra*, an iron collier of the Cintra Steam Navigation Company of Liverpool, out of Newport for Dartmouth. Meeting with rough weather, her captain anchored in Carbis Bay, with seven fathoms under his keel. It was four in the morning. After a while, Captain Green ups his anchor again to come inshore to St Ives to telegraph his company. By then, the *Vulture* is in trouble in the Bay, as is the *Bessie*. The lifeboat maroons go off, and the men begin to haul for the two gigs, the *Bessie* and the *Boy Philip*, which are stuck on Gwithian. It was then that the captain set out against heavy seas; they were crashing aboard and took off ventilators and bent every bit of iron they could. All those waves did for her windlass and jammed the chain. The crew ran out from the shelter of the bridge to try each time to shift the chain with hammers and chisels. God knows why! It was well and truly stuck. The captain had nothing for it then but to hoist a distress signal and get the lifeboat over the side. He lost four of his men when it capsized. The *Cintra* was going onto the beach where the rest of the crew got off with the help of the coastguard; two of them died an hour after they got ashore.

A hundred feet offshore, the *Cintra* was breaking up. We did not know then that the *Hampshire* was sinking ten miles north of Godrevy. A crankshaft broke loose in the engine-room and tore a hole in the bilges. She went down an hour later. The captain and fourteen of his crew drowned.

In those days, some would go to the sands and grieve the loss of loved ones. They paid no heed that the sea was up to their knees.

I was tired, looking forward to my bed, when I heard the rockets again. I got my oilskin on and went out. This time it was a steamship in trouble. I fought my way against the wind to Wharf Road, as the sea took her on past the harbour mouth. 'He will try to beach her on Porthminster,' said Sam Cleave. 'They've got the lifeboat out into open water, but they won't do nothing against that sea.'

It was rough there where we stood, so we cut up through Cocking Court into Fore Street. We ran through the Market, on by the church to St Andrew and up behind Pedn Olva. There, on the rocks, we could see the lifeboat, cast up, her oars broken. The crew had made her fast to get ashore and climb to safety. The coastguard lads had already gotten down to the beach from the station above, and were about to fire a line on board. The steamship was coming broadside on to land.

'He did well to get her ashore in one piece, but I can't see she'll lay that way for long,' said Sam. 'She's leaking water at every hole it can find. She'll be fit for nothing but scrap shortly.'

Coming back, I saw one of the crew kneeling in the lee of the church. Soon as he saw me, he got up and was making to go when I said, 'Are you lost, Christian?' I could see that he was dazed.

He said the *Rosedale* was out of Southampton, and had met with foul weather coming round the Head to go up to Cardiff. The Captain had no choice but to bring her into the bay and try to ground her.

'You got nowhere in mind to go, you better come home along with me,' I said. 'We'll soon put something warm in your belly. Come on now, you don't have far to go.'

I recall Susan stood at the cellar door in the fading light. She held a hurricane lamp; a sash weight fell from her hand, and rang as it rolled down the cobbles of the hill. I never knew why she was out at that time, or what she was doing with the sash weight. I had told her to go to bed.

The storm meant there were no early trains across the dunes at Carbis Bay. The spume was still coming ashore in yellow curds. When they abated at last, the *Rosedale* lay over to starboard. To my mind she was in enough of one piece to float off at high water. That was not to be, though; I was wrong. She was full of water, and the weather staying wild, she was left to fall apart.

By then, they had built the West Pier, and were using it to

load roadstone from the quarry. It was a fixed-light gas burner that shone green when there were less than ten feet of water at the pier head. I forget the number of degrees.

I had Richard Taylor and James Stevens come in my store. When they were boys they had a rusty bike they shared that had no saddle. I gave them one, and oil for the rust. In those days, boys were boys and not sent to torment my life. When I was their age I was at sea. What they were after then, was to sell brass fittings. I knew where they had got them, and I said, 'You been out there on the *Rosedale*.'

'You want this brass or not?'

That was James Stevens; then Richard Taylor said, 'Let him go hang. We can sell these easy enough in Penzance.'

I stowed the brass in one of the bags of bones. I gave them less than it was worth, because I had a feeling at the back of my mind they would get me into trouble. Sure enough, they fell to boasting about it over in the Sloop. Next thing I know Sergeant Jones come in my stores asking have I bought any brass recently. I said no, worried that he might root out my hiding place there and then. Of course, I had not put anything down about brass in my record book. Soon as he went away the best thing to do, I thought, was to take it to Penzance quick as I could.

I set off early the next day, feeling the more relieved the further I got from St Ives. Sergeant Jones is a dogged man. He was there, coming at me along the street on his bicycle, just as I got to Denley's. 'I knew you might come here today,' he said, smiling.

When he asked for brass, I said no, and showed him copper pipe. He leaned his bike against the wall, took off his clips and pulled a notebook out of his tunic. I was sick of it all; he was taking it in such good part, in that easygoing way he has, that I said, 'Bugger it, Mr Jones, you deserve the truth pushing that bike over to here,' and I threw the bag of bones down in the street.

I was in the dock at the St Ives Borough Police Court on a charge of receiving stolen goods. If I had not had the ten pounds in hand to pay the fine I would have gone to Bodmin Prison sure. Neither of those lads could pay the twenty-five shillings, so they got a month in gaol. I would not wish my worst enemy a day in Bodmin.

I heard that soldiers were on the Island. They were knocking down the old gun battery. I thought I would walk up there to see if there was anything in it for me. It was a grand spot for drying nets. Spread them out on the grass and you could roll them up dry again in no time.

Two soldiers were sitting among pickaxes, shovels and crowbars, a bread loaf and two tins of sardines between them. One was called Otway; the other did not have much to say for himself. I said, 'You got nothing here in the scrap metal line you want rid of, then?'

Otway shook his head. 'Even if you could see anything we could make a bob on, it would be more than our lives are worth to let you have it. We got an officer who hates St Ives. Driving him mad, he says, so he will never miss a chance to give us hell about a button undone.'

'Why is this called the Island, when it isn't one?' His mate had his mouth full.

'It was an island one time, then tides shifted the sand behind it and made a spit of land,' I said. 'It took a long time, but that's how things happen.'

I looked across and saw a ship in the bay. She was a queer mixture, like so many coastal boats that were once deep-sea goers. She had the look of a schooner about her, but with a mast missing while the bowsprit carried a cluster of jibsails.

I told Otway that I thought she would take a lot of handling. The helmsman was good, though; he had brought her up to the wind tidy so that the sails began to flutter and she lay still. I could hear the pawls clanking on the windlass as the hook went down.

'Her captain does not want to be stuck in harbour until the next tide,' I said.

Otway took out a telescope. 'Why are they getting a longboat over the side? Are they after a pilot?'

I laughed. I could see it all in a flash. After you left the Bay of Biscay, you came east along the Channel. On the turn there was where you might need a *Seaman's Guide and Coaster's Companion*. You read that and it will tell you to make land about the Lizard, if you can. Going from there to the Start, you must never have less than forty fathoms under you, for you are in the Eddystone stream. Keep to that depth, and you will be in no danger. If you fall too far south and mistake the Casket Lights for Portland, you are in trouble. It is a place that has been fatal to many a ship. If a good skipper has any seamanship about him, he can bring a clipper past the Goodwins, round Margate headland, and be well past the Reculvers Mark up the Thames estuary before he calls for a tugboat.

'You know about sailing, then?' I said.

'Look out, here comes Inchcape,' said Otway's mate, setting his cap straight as he stood to attention.

Inchcape came on at a trot soon as he saw I was there, saying, 'You are trespassing on War Office property, you've got no business here.'

I told him that half St Ives came up there to dry their nets; they were doing that before he was born.

I was going anyway; that longboat would soon be ashore, and I wanted to know why it had come. Turned out that a crewman had been taken sick, and they were bringing him to see a doctor. I heard he died later; his appendix burst.

After that, I went round to meet Susan. She had gone to Academy Place to see how Bessie was doing. I met her on the steps there, by the Zion Chapel. She said that Bessie was going to give birth any day now, and she had said for her to come stay at Bethesda Hill. Jacob had a son he called after him, and Bessie died eight days later. With her gone, Jacob and the babe moved in to live with us.

Mrs Bryant came knocking, one bleak November day. Her husband had sent her to tell us that the gig *Fortitude* had been out fishing in the bay and had run into trouble. The tug *Energy* got a line aboard her, but the tow broke, off Carrack Gladden Point.

'It's fearsome out there, poor things,' said Susan.

The four of them tried to run her aground on Western Spits, Mrs Bryant said, but she overturned. Three men went over the side. The skipper's nephew had to cut himself free of ropes and gear to get up the beach. Nobody heard his cries; the other three were swept away. He walked to Lelant to knock on a door there. They gave him dry clothes, and he took the train home to St Ives. The dead men were Mr Matthew Freeman, the skipper, William Paul and James Uren Long.

Sometimes it seemed as if the Angel of Death was forever flying over the town. The death of Bessie brought Jacob very low. He would say nothing at all for months. Nancy Bryant was touched to see him drag about the town with his postbag. She said he was in need of a wife to care for the children, so she married him, and they went to live up-along Island Road.

★

We got off early for Penzance to see General Booth. At seventy-five, old Billy had his mind set to go pell-mell from Land's End to Aberdeen in a Humber motor car.

Susan had her black straw bonnet and tunic on, I had my Sunday best and I brushed my bowler. Soon as our shadows fell on them, bright red admirals rose out of the furze. Butterflies were aflitter all along the path. Maybe the breeze had brought them there, and they were having a rest.

Us were walking at a fair old clip. She strides so fast I have to scuttle to keep up with her mutter, muttering along.

Soon as we got there, Susan was off to talk to Army women – and try to get near the General, I knew. I saw it as a way she did not have to tell anybody I was her husband.

I saw Mr Swail come along the street to sneak a look. He used to be a shipwright and still went about in his old work clothes: jacket without a collar, a moleskin apron, blue serge trousers with a long pocket for a rule – you never saw him without one of those. Always had a red sweat rag hanging out of his back pocket. He had worked on ships in Cheshire, Liverpool and London. He was too fond of his booze even to think about signing any Article of War.

'Five cars,' said Mr Swail, putting on his steel-rimmed glasses. 'The General I can see, but who are all these other buggers, Alf?'

I told him the names of the Evangelist's Apostles: Commissioners Cadman, Coombs and Nicol, with Colonel Lawley and Colonel Eadie.

'Who are all these others, then?'

'The Mayor and such like – reporters for the *War Cry* and every other paper, I suppose,' I said.

'People have turned out all right. I've not seen such a crush since Mafeking night.'

A woman I had not seen for a long time came along selling

the *War Cry*. I knew her face, red as a brick, with blue eyes. She knew me, but I had forgotten her name and kept trying to call it to mind. 'I hear the actor, Sir Henry Irving, is here somewhere,' she said with a laugh. 'Where? Our General has put him quite in the shade.'

She had been at meetings, but not for a while. She had not seen Mrs Wallis. Was she there somewhere about? She must be. She had much to tell her. How she was living in Fowey now, and was going on a mission to China. She did so miss hearing me play my melodion. She had always enjoyed that. She had been down at Land's End with the General, and had watched him go with Mr Begbie to the very edge of the cliff, where he spoke the words 'Lo, on this narrow neck of land,' from Wesley's hymn. Did I know that Wesley had been moved to write it there? What a lion of a man our General was! He was so old, yet still fought bravely at the heart of things. From there, he had gone to the chapel in St Just, a scene of his former triumph. 'You will read all about it in the next *War Cry*. Buy one now! It has it all: we sell the *War Cry* to both the Russians and the Japanese at war in Manchuria. We are planting the flag everywhere, from German Africa to Jamaica and Palestine!'

She went off waving the paper. Swail smiled. He had lost a few front teeth, his face burnt copper by the sea and wind, white skin showing only in his open shirt. 'These flying visits!' he said. 'We both know there's as much backsliding as zeal in this place, Alf. You don't often get down this way. How are you liking St Ives?'

'I got no standing in that town, and never will have any except with a few people,' I said. 'I find it hard to call many friends. I never make those easy.'

I showed him a photograph of the business. I had moved to the Wharf by then. I forget who did it. Mr Preston came with his camera from Penzance, and was taking pictures everywhere. It may have been him, Mr Dryden or Mr Ashton was here with his – or again, Mr Armour had a camera. Whoever did it, it came out very well, I thought. 'You can't see me because I was behind the cart,' I said. 'That's Albert in the shafts. I sort cottons from woollens all day, if you feel like walking over.' Maybe he would see more of me, anyway. I knew how Italians made ice cream. There was plenty of ice in St Ives, and I was going to get over to Penzance with a barrow to sell the ice cream there of a weekend.

Susan came up to say that General Booth looked weary enough already, even before he got started. He was planning to visit sixty-two cities and hold three or more meetings every day. All the people around St Just had followed him everywhere.

'Billy Booth can talk to black and white the world over, and to kings and queens,' I said to Mr Swail. 'They understand his message in Limehouse, and so do five thousand Zulus in darkest Africa.'

'Penzance is dear to the General's heart,' Susan said; 'his son Herbert was born here.'

After that, General Billy Booth had a mad attraction for vehicles at large. He was never out of one. Canopy up in all weathers, his white beard aflying from under his motoring cape, he went racing through England, Scotland and Wales. He was in a hansom cab coming away from a railway station once when a wheel came off. He walked away from that wreck. Then, the next year, he was in Jerusalem on his knees under an olive tree in the Garden of Gethsemane.

I was always amazed he lived as long as he did.

It was in all the papers about how Peary and Matthew

Henson had got to the North Pole. Or did they? Had Doctor Cook got there first? Peary came ashore on Labrador to say that Cook was a fraud. They were ever at it then – one after the other, expeditions went out, drawn to seek the ends of the earth.

And all that motoring had taken it out of General Booth. We didn't know until later but they had operated on a cataract in his right eye. He got an abscess under there, and lost it altogether. It was not long before his left eye put him out of the firing line. He wrote a letter to the *War Cry* that had Susan in tears; he was blind. Then the paper said he was poorly; three days later, after a thunderstorm, he laid down his sword.

Susan read out that on a Thursday in August seven thousand Salvationists and forty bands went a five-mile march around London to Abney Park in Stoke Newington to lay him to rest. He had stopped the traffic in the City of London an hour and a half. Sixty-five thousand people had gone up to see him in his coffin.

Sorry, I got to wipe my eyes; they leak worse now than they ever did, no matter what the weather. The wind at sea did for them, I expect.

What am I making? This is gazpacho – I ate it in Spain: chop up half a cucumber, some onions and tomatoes. I grow the garlic in a bucket. You don't get colds if you eat plenty of garlic. Susan never liked the smell.

I put the turkshead over the side to fend her bow off the pier. Down in the clear water, pilchard fry dart under the keel into the shadow in the last of the light. Moths fly around the lighthouse above, shining out already across the bay. A blind man – I do not know him – runs his white stick along the edge of the quay as he leans over. 'Where away,' he says. 'You need a hand?'

What can I say? He sends his stick handle down. 'Hang a line on that. I know the bollard's here.'

'If you're sure,' I say. I was so afraid, I did not want to speak a word to him.

Hand over hand, I got up the steel rungs onto the pier.

'You coming along, Alf?' It was Joshua going by.

'Directly.'

The blind man nodded as though he could see him. 'No luck, eh?'

'No.'

After a silence, the blind man said, 'I would like nothing better than to be in your shoes. I spend all my time near the sea when I can afford it, or have the leisure.'

He said he had gone blind when he was a child. He never liked to think about it, but could remember how his mother used to read him *Robinson Crusoe*. He was quite natural the way he fell into talking about the first thing Crusoe did on seeing the footprint, never mind that it was clearly made by a man. 'Fear,' he said. 'Crusoe's instinct is to run home fast as a fox to his earth, afraid they will destroy his corn and steal his goats. He digs a wall outside his cave and aims his seven muskets ready to fire them all off in two minutes. We know him so well, never mind how wrong he is. I used to think I could smell those old goatskins he wore.' Then, after a moment, he went on, 'A man will use his eyes as if there were no end to his seeing, then, one day, he wakes up and finds he's blind.'

'You want anything, apart to pass the time of day?'

'Will you go out again tomorrow?' I heard him catch a breath. 'Can I come with you?'

'Don't know about that,' I said.

34

'I'd sit where I was told. I'd be no bother. I wouldn't say a word unless somebody spoke first.'

'Taking a passenger is not something I can decide myself. There are the others. They might say it was bad luck having you aboard. We got to put it to a show of hands, and they will want payment of some sort.'

'I can afford that, if it's reasonable,' he said. 'Are you for or against it?'

'Why do you ask?'

'I feel I can trust you to plead my case.'

I told him to be early for high water in the morning. Did he know what time that was?

Sam did not relish the fact that he was blind. Josh did not like the black leather glove the man wore on his left hand. 'What's wrong with it? What is he hiding under it?' Jim Hesp was too young to vote.

A foghorn sounded in the bay as a ship passed. A thick mist hid the harbour. I could hear the plash of oars, voices calling out, wood striking wood. Across on the West Pier, a donkey engine got going after a slow start. The sound soon changed as it began to lift a weight. The first load of quarry stone rumbled into the hold. The sun shone white in the haze. Soon, it began to burn it off until you could see Tregenna Hill above the Malakoff, then the top of the church tower. Lower yet, the masts came into sight. When I could make them out, the men were faint ghosts.

The blind man sat waiting by the hard, chin atop his hands on his stick. He had found a jersey, a pair of corduroy trousers, and had an oilskin under his arm. He said the others had gone on ahead; he had told them he would wait for me.

I took his arm and sat him down in the boat, then pushed

off to scull to where the *Agnes* lay. Shipping the oar, I hopped aboard to make the rope fast as the dinghy ran aft. Then I hauled it in, and we helped him on deck. I could feel the air begin to freshen.

They told him their names: Josh, Sam, and the boy, Jim.

'Mine is A. J. Mortly,' he said.

'Nothing shorter than that?'

'Arthur will do.'

'Wet your finger, Alf, or we're going nowhere,' said Sam. 'Any sign it'll stir?'

The sails were chill with dew as we untied them. Sam and I got up on the quay, where I undid the hawser. We walked with it across our shoulders to haul her head out into open water.

You know, no matter what time you take a boat out, that somebody has his eye on you. They watch every move you make, and will tell you where you were at fault soon as you get back – if you do get back. They are saying you will not. You can't spit in these parts without running into a lawgiver. You would think they could walk on water. Every current here is deep, and you can run foul of one before you know it. Too clever by half, they will say, and those are words that can shrink a man.

It was just after high water, the tide was already on the turn and took the *Agnes* out fast into the bay where the wind soon filled the sails. It was chiller than we had thought. I had not a lot to say, and Sam is never much of a one for talking. The herring-gulls and black-backs were yelping and screeching to give a noisy send-off as they flew out with us.

'We fish fifty miles north of the Head, but we're not going out that far,' I said. 'We'll line-fish today, see what we can get.'

What we do, I told him, was to put three lines out – port

and starboard, and one astern. Getting a mackerel hooked when it's a hot day, we try everything. We pull a line up, then let it down again; you couldn't say how many times. 'You leave a mackerel on the line as a teaser, let the others come and chase that. I go hooking fish only when I got nothing better to do,' I said.

We found a net was torn in places, so we hauled it up the mast and set-to to mend it as we went along.

Mr Tregurtha hailed us half a mile off, his voice carrying across. 'Be careful how you go, there's squid about,' was what I made out of what he said, holding up a net to show the hole they must have torn.

'I've known squids to stoit six feet into a boat, come flying out of the air,' said Joshua.

Jim's pennyworth was, 'Why squid is tough is that it's all muscle so that it can race backwards through the sea.'

That got him a few laughs. Jim was a truant from school, but he was where he wanted to be in life.

When Mr Mortly asked about sharks, I told him you saw them now and then. They were not worth the fight to get them out of the water. 'Sharks have pilot fish that go with them everywhere, striped creatures about as big as perch,' I said. 'In tropic latitudes, sharks will dog a vessel for days. They have to go over on their back to strike a man, to get him in their mouth.'

We were some miles along the coast and making good headway when Joshua said, 'There is plenty of sea room. There'd be no harm in Mr Mortly taking a turn for five minutes.'

'You will feel the wind on your face,' I told Mr Mortly. 'All you need do is set the tiller over and hold hard against it. Sing out, if you don't think you can hold her.'

Mr Mortly had a smile as pleased as Mr Punch. It was a

37

good thing he could not see Jim's face when he began to call him young Hawkins.

Just after sundown, son, he said, when young Hawkins was about to go to his berth, he had an urge to eat an apple. The forward watch was looking for the island, and the helmsman had an eye to the sails as he listened. It was the only sound, apart from the sea alongside the *Hispaniola*. The stock of apples was low, and Jim had to get into the barrel to find one. There, the gentle rolling of the ship sent him to sleep. It was not until Long John Silver sat down and nudged the barrel with his shoulder that he woke up.

'I'm not your son. You call me Jim Hesp,' Jim warned. 'Anything else, you got it wrong.'

Joshua laughed. 'Pay no mind. He's been on boats since he could walk; you got the tiller, and that's put his nose out of joint.'

It was only by the power of reason that we were out at sea at all, said Mr Mortly. Men had first to learn about tools and timber, then the ways of wind, weather and navigation. All those skills they got from their fathers, who in turn had them from theirs. He said we all came from the sea, and it was with us until we died. We could taste the salt in our tears. It took us millions of years, but we got ashore after some fashion, then up into the trees.

'Are you trying to say that God is not in Genesis, that he did not make it all in six days? We are all godfearing aboard this vessel,' Joshua warned. 'You may have suffered in your time, but we are all strict men here. There are doors we open, and those we keep shut.'

The argument had taken this serious turn, and nobody had a mind to anything else. Mortly stood up when he felt the change and heard the boom swing over. In the rush for the helm we all got in the way of each other, yet none of us was frantic enough to reach that tiller in time. Mortly fell in the bottom of the boat, nursing his knee, which had caught a kick. A cross-tide coming off the headland and a shift in the wind had the *Agnes* firmly. Her head had found its way over and her tail was following. 'We are going inshore; no other way for it,' I said.

We ran aground in no time. Reefing the sail, we threw a hook over the side to wait for high water again.

'Is it serious?' Mr Mortly stared up at me.

'You were never in charge of the wind or the tide,' I said.

Joshua stared out at the headland, then finally shook his head. 'I was sure I knew it all about this coast, where every current ran.'

'Bugger! Bugger! Bugger it!' said Jim.

'I'll hear no bad language on here, Jim, and you know that,' Joshua warned. 'She's come to rest easy enough now. We're stuck fast until nightfall now, and even then the wind has to come round.'

There was nothing to see up on the cliff top, only gulls riding the wind. There was no mine chimney, no steps or anything else.

Sam began to rig an awning; the sun was hot in the shelter of the cove.

'You would have done better, Jim, if you had been in charge,' said Mr Mortly, still feeling bad.

Jim had nothing to say. It was hot, so he took off his shirt and pants and dived over the side.

I set off to climb the cliff. Half-way up, the path became steeper. With the sun blazing so, I sat down to rest. Jim had come out of the sea, and sat naked with the surf breaking against him. Then he got up and began to run east towards the cliff.

Sam had left the boat and was walking the other way with an axe. I could not make out what he was doing, except he swung the axe down on the rocks, but Joshua knew at once. 'He's killing seals,' he said. 'He got in close; they don't see well at all.'

All the seals were dead by the time we got back except three that had swum off. Mortly was silent. His day out had left the taste of ashes in his mouth. He must have heard the killing of the seals, the wailing of the pups. He would know something awful was going on but could not tell what it was. He would hear Sam go off along the rocks, and he would smell blood on him when he came back and heard the axe thud on the deck.

They had got up on the rocks to bask there until high water again. There was a bull hauled out, too, but he had been too old to do much about it. One was an albino. Sam was bloody as a cannibal, stuck with chips of bone. He had to take off his clothes and get into the sea before we let him come aboard. I went over and saw the pup that had a white coat. There were flies on it already, but it was trying to lift its head. I hit it hard to kill it.

'You didn't kill the pup,' said Jim.

'Soon as I killed one,' Sam said, 'the mother stood her ground and came to lunge at me. I let the other go – without her milk it won't last long.'

'You made a right mess of it out there,' I said.

'It's a war, Alf, you know. Never mind the fairy stories. You seen them go after fish in our nets, you've mended holes they tear.'

I thought Mr Mortly foolhardy to say what he did, that

40

they were going to put a bill through Parliament to protect the grey seal.

'Grey, white or brown, they are all the same to me,' said Sam. 'My father would always kill one, soon as he saw it. He always carried a gaff aboard, a spike on a club that went straight into the brain.'

He had the taste now for talking about it, knowing that it would upset Mr Mortly. The pups had been asleep when he started; they must have tired themselves out going after squid. They were good for nothing now; the tide would wash them out. Crabs and eels could get into them easy now; he had cut enough gashes.

'It was nothing but your rage you took out on those dumb creatures,' I said.

Sam was never soft. I have seen him drown a litter of pups in a tub of water, and I never liked the slow way he did it.

'I'm sorry I ran the boat aground,' said Mr Mortly, feeling he was to blame for the whole thing.

Mr Judd's pig broke free and ran down the Digey; children were after it, falling over each other in the hue and cry. Their shrieks and halloos only made the poor creature run the faster. Dogs, too, joined in the excitement. It ran into the harbour and swam out until a fisherman got hold of its ear. The children tied a rope to its back leg and hauled it up the hill to where Mr Judd stood with a knife in one hand and a kettle to scald it when it was dead. Some of them got the bladder to blow up when he killed it. I went up there as he was salting the meat and bought a hind leg from him. It was sweetly cured. There was nothing you could tell Mr Judd about pigs. He was a dab hand at keeping them.

Susan was grieving then for Emily, who had died. Things were changing quicker than a man could keep up with. It was bad enough then, before 1907, when fishermen sold their boats to Mr Denley for as little as a pound, and it got worse. Trade's always taking a new turn, and those turns never seem other than to work against poor men and drive them to the wall. Grimsby, Lowestoft, Yarmouth had become the towns for fish. They had steam trawlers to scour the North Sea, taking cod, haddock, crabs, and codlings, spawn and all. They came here, too, to do men out of a living. The Newlyn men saw red and got up in arms – those North Sea buggers were fishing all the hours God sent. Sundays, too, they went out to cast their nets. We tied a rope across the harbour; we beat those buggers on sight, and threw their fish back in the sea. Then the Penzance boys got in the fight alongside the Lowestoft men, so there were armed soldiers marching about to keep the peace when pilchards were in season. They had a man o' war anchored out there, too. We soon had to go clear up to Scotland to fish. If we had a bit of luck, a good catch – by the time we got it ashore the price would be against us, and we had to throw it over the side.

It all stood or fell by what the sea would let us take. Some went to America, some down the mines; others set off to petition Parliament for engines. Not until the war did they get those, when the Kaiser's warships had the East Coast fleets shut up in port. Even then, there was no way out for any of us. Most of the Porthmeor seine boats had gone.

It's no good banking on the sea; it can undo you. Where are the pilchards now? The Lord provideth, and He taketh away. Families then had to live on credit where they could get it.

The *Susan Elizabeth* went under in a tempest coming home here. Joshua Daniel owned her, the coal merchant. All that was left of her to see was the wind tearing the topsail to shreds. She was a schooner but had been built as a cutter. I said to Mr Hesp as we stood, 'Two waves will wreck a ship: one throws her ashore, the other smashes her to match-wood.' Her master was John Curnow, and it was the second time he had lost a ship at St Ives. The last was a schooner called the *Jasper*. Where the *Susan Elizabeth* lay, she was in the way of the seine-fishing, and they had to blow her up in October. By then, they found a live turtle had come aboard her.

It was another chill morning in January when William came over from Penzance to tell us that Charlie was dead. I walked out on Clodgy. When I'm there sometimes, I think I hear the tolling of a hundred and forty sunken church bells of Lyonesse all the way to the Scilly Isles, as lost as my mother. There was never much to do on those islands except wreck ships or pack flowers, so my mother went into service in Penzance.

With Charlie dead, there was another end. I could not find it in my heart, though, to forgive him. My mother's brother Uncle Ellis had gone off to Australia and did well, rising to be captain of a goldmine. Being a true believer, as he grew older he set about thinking who would get his fortune. I had no notion that Charlie wrote to him, and kept him in the dark about my whereabouts. He said he had not heard of me for years, although I was there, living under his roof every time I came ashore. Brotherly love flies out the window when it comes down to the wherewithal.

'The Lord made him my brother,' I said to Susan, 'now He has seen fit to punish him for all that he did against me, but I have to try to find forgiveness in my heart.'

I hired two motor cars to take us all to bury Charlie. If General Booth could ride in those, so could I. I was with

Susan, Albert and his wife Margaret; Thomas Williams and Jessie, Jacob and Nancy Bryant and their children rode in the other.

That car left thick smoky fumes behind, but the air around was sweet as cold milk. You ride easy in a car on such a day; you got nothing to think about except old grievances, how the past could happen the way it did.

I was living in Penzance with Charlie and Father till Father died. He had been a master paver before he went for a soldier to the Crimea. God knows how he did not catch cholera. If you got cholera, you shat yourself to death in short order. It ran out of you until it was only water, and that water was your living substance. Our soldiers came down with it like flies. They wasted away until they were a bag of bones to bury.

Charlie was still living in Gas Court. He was all set to bury Father in Penzance until I put my foot down. I said he was going home to Devonport to lie beside our mother.

We got the coffin to the station. It took two porters to get it into the van. Soon as the guard came in, Charlie offered him a swig of brandy, which he said he would not take because he was on duty. I said we were to stay with Father, and he said no, that was against regulations as well. In the end, he said there were only the fish boxes to sit on, anyway, but he had plenty of old newspapers.

'It's what he would have wanted,' I said. 'Any road, it's what I want, Charlie.'

Father had wanted a better life for us all, but that was never in his gift. When he was dying upstairs he would shout commands, sure that his mates were about to be killed. That war in the Crimea had changed him; war does change a man. Thank God, I never had to go to one.

When father came home, he was missing some of his

friends; those that did get back would never want to talk about it. A lot of the time he was digging earth behind wicker hurdles for defences, glad of them when the grapeshot burst. When I asked him, he could never think of a reason why he was there at all. None of it did any good – all that mud, those semaphores flashing night and day, horses going by he never knew where or why to be cut to pieces with their riders. He was a slow man, not too quick at picking things up, so the officers were always shouting and down on him.

'Shit, shit, shit, it's all shit, Alfred,' Charlie said, 'and that you have always been full of. You never could shake that off, even when you went to sea. All of us are going to come to this, a body in a coffin; nobody cares at all what you did.'

'Just because it's true, you don't have to say it.'

'You know what I got, Alf, same as Mother had, so I know I'm not long for this world.'

'Drink won't help that,' I said.

'No, nothing will.'

Strong liquor had been the scourge of all my family, and Charlie had come to it, too. Even then, he had drunk too much. It would either get worse as time wore on, or he would fall asleep.

At nightfall, when I leaned out of the train, the stars hung bright and clear and I could see the firebox glow under the chimney smoke.

At Mother's grave in Devonport the next day, Charlie was still not sober.

All this I kept trying to hold in my mind going in the car, with Susan sat beside me, stiff as a poker. She could not get over it that her sons and daughters had lost a fortune. 'If you hate him so much, why are you putting on this show with motor cars? All those times he came creeping around corners in St Ives to buy scrap, and took the bread out of our mouths!'

Ever since she had known Charlie, he had always been short-sighted and deceitful, she said.

'That Lizzie put him up to it, it was her who has been against us all along. He would not have the spunk to do it himself. They are both of them the same. Tell me when was she ever sober! I can't ever forget her shouting at me to get up there to Men-an-Tol after Ellen Jane died. "Go crawl in that hole nine times against the sun, same as any low trash, to get your dry old womb to bear fruit!" '

'All we can say is that when Uncle Ellis died they never went short again,' I said.

She grew vexed and heated. 'What was Billy asaying to you?'

'The old tale. He was on again about his father had nothing to do with it all; that Uncle Ellis heard about Charlie's drinking and cut him out of his will; that Rowe got the fifty thousand pounds. He talks about hiring a lawyer.'

'Billy is crafty. He wants your blessing,' she said. 'He lives in hope that you will say he is nothing like his father, but leopards don't change their skins.'

Had I got a share in that fortune, I would not be living hand to mouth now, scrimping to stay out of the workhouse, living in fear of lying in a pauper's grave. All families will founder when money comes into the picture; they scrap like dogs over a bone.

There were flags by the grave, and the wind set one reed spiralling and left all the rest. It seemed always to strike the same place. I could time it coming and going; but just when I thought I had the measure of it, a flurry came that blew them all about. Then it dropped back to idle and twist the one flag again. I had to say it then, 'He was our Charlie,

Mother, yours and mine; you could feel his silence when he was out to look at birds. He loved those birds. If it had not been for Lizzie, we would never have fallen out.'

I had nothing to say to her. I could smell the drink on her breath as she went by, and I wondered it had not killed her by now.

By the cemetery gate, Mr Denley stopped to catch his breath. He had done nothing to dress up to pay his respects. I have never cared for that snuff-brown handkerchief he used all the time. 'Even as we stand here, there might be riches underfoot, Mr Wallis,' he said. 'We don't know, now do we?'

'What do you mean, Mr Denley?'

'Two years ago, when they were digging to lay the Heamoor water main between the cricket field and us, they broke into an old mine.' He sighed. 'Nobody knows everything, and no miner living could recall those workings. I know, because I went around asking.'

Mr Denley himself said how fast things were changing now. He had been to Camborne to an auction of mining gear, and they had a tram there he rode on.

'It all passes away, and our flesh goes with it.'

That month was a bad one for storms and wrecks. Three days after we buried Charlie two ships were driven ashore at St Ives. At nine o'clock, a big three-mast, topsail schooner, the *Lizzie B. Wilce,* heading for St Mâlo, fell foul of Porthminster beach. No sooner had the lifeboat crew got their heads down than more flares were seen rising off a collier, the schooner *Mary Barrow.* The coastguard's rocket broke on the mainmast, but they got her crew ashore in the lifeboat. She came to rest not two hundred yards from the other schooner. They got her afloat a week later and towed her to Leah's yard at Falmouth.

★

I came down Fish Street and saw two men and a woman standing on the top step, talking by the gaslight. You could feel the grit of sand underfoot that had been walked along the street. A soft breeze was blowing, and the woman was holding her hat with one hand and her skirt with the other. I could hear a fiddle. I knew Mr Tregurtha was playing it; that it was white with rosin, he would go at it so long. There were drums and a mandolin as well, for the dance up there. As I turned the corner, I heard a ruction going on. Back-along then, the sand came up to the wall of the Sloop, and so did the sea in bad weather. Two big fisher lads had a gypsy against the wall of the alehouse. I knew their names. I could smell the liquor on their breath, and saw the man they were beating clearly in the light from the window. He was shouting, 'You bastards! All of you bastards, I'll kill you dead!'

A third man turned and warned, 'You fuck off now, Old Iron; you hear?'

The gypsy broke free and ran crouching across the road. They caught him and knocked him down on the sand, shouting, 'You go making eyes at our women, you know what you'll get. We'll break every fucking bone in your body.'

With that, they were knocking him out into the water of the harbour.

'Let him up out of that; you'll drown the bugger else,' said Hesp. 'He's had his lesson. You want to swing for him?'

'Best you get off home, Mr Wallis,' said Arthur Judd. 'Don't be standing there, where they might call you to speak up against anybody.'

Suddenly I could see Tighe; a man too big for me to fight, but that is what he was after. I had nowhere to run. His first blow hit my belly, and I was a fish out of water. Could not

48

get breath at all into my hurt lungs. I thought my heart had stopped, and that it would never start. As I lifted my head, Tighe hit me above my left eye. I don't recall a lot after that. When I came to, the sun was flashing in my eyes each time the sail fell limp. I sat up and wiped my bloody mouth. They told me I saved myself by biting half his ear off.

Soon as the lads had gone, I crept over to the gypsy and found him lying on his side with his knees drawn up. I feared he was dead, but when I came nearer I heard him groan. He got up. 'You get off now,' he said, but as soon as he opened his mouth blood ran out.

I did as I was told. I went home and gave myself a treat: a big spoonful of treacle.

I saw him the next day. His nose was split open; somebody had stitched the cut on his left cheek with black thread and made it look worse. I was amazed to see him in the town at all, and thought that he might have some sort of knife or weapon on him. Maybe he was out for revenge on those lads who beat him. Well, he was unlucky; they were fishing. Later on, a woman came along with a basket of pegs. She wasn't selling them; she was looking for him.

The Wards came knocking to tell us all about the coronation of George V they had seen at the Picturedrome, which had opened up Barnoon way. Jessie was taken with the conjurer who did a turn in the interval, and was a ventriloquist too. Not long after that, I shut down the business. I baled up the last of the rags, tossed the chains and scrap together on the cart, and got help to load my scales aboard. I felt well shot of it all, and wished Mr Denley well of the lot. Mind you, people knew to come and bring stuff to Back Road. If I saw anything I could turn a shilling on, I'd buy it. I would store it up until Denley got over to fetch it. In the passage outside, here and there, anywhere I could find room.

Susan had buried a lot of her children then. The dates are all here in the family Bible – her son George in 1895. The other children had left home, Jacob a postman and Albert a baker. Of the girls, only Jessie was alive, married to Mr Williams' son, who was also a fisherman. So I thought we would have no trouble living on what I'd put by. Neither of us would die for want in the street. I could never rid myself of the fear of falling sick or lame. I would die rather than know she was shut up in one crib while I was in another and some overseer come in to tell me she was dead. Afraid, too, of her being cut up like a dead horse, or a dog in a kennel.

Susan was seventy-eight – I was fifty-six. Two rooms would be ample for us, so I had already bought the cottage in Back Road West. Susan had her pension, and I did odd jobs for Mr Armour in his antique shop. We did not need much. She was a dab hand at cutting my hair. For oilskins, I would stand still for her to fix the canvas shapes she cut to fit my body; then, when they were sewn, she had oil boiling to dip the suit. If I did need a jersey, she bought fourteen ounces of dark blue worsted wool to knit one with four needles. She had a stuffed pad she tied around her waist to take the weight of the wool. Had no need of a pattern, she made it up as she went along. See how they wear; this is one of hers.

We had forty pounds in gold and five pounds in silver in a chest upstairs, more than enough for our coffins and burial plot. Susan would beat the doormat on the wall outside first thing, then she would brush the road in front of the house clean, the sweeper's job. She kept it all spotless. Mrs Peters used to come to see how Susan was doing when I was on a job for Mr Armour or out shopping. Old Sun's wife, Mrs Phillips, sold eggs. She had poultry along there.

When the war came, I went up on the Island to build huts for the government. There used to be a shrine to St Eia up there, which had a light for sailors at night. Then it became a store, and the army knocked it down. Sir Edward Hain built the Nicholas Chapel when George V was crowned.

Susan kept her dolly-tub and wringer in the scullery, behind that screen. Nobody can know the pleasure I get from that stuffed magpie on the mantelshelf. This is the couch I sleep on now, our old chairs, one round table, one square, black, with the white porcelain knob. I cover that with a newspaper when I paint. I got a dresser, some books – that dark-green one is Whittier's poems. I have the earth lavatory behind I empty of a night down Porthmeor.

Soon as they made a start on Wharf Road, the war came. They didn't get to it again until the year Susan was dying.

Anywhere there's fish there's cats. Pudding-bag-lane had more than its fair share of them. I had a cat aboard ship once when I was young. I used to fish for it until it got washed overboard. It didn't run fast enough. I heard it cry, it knew what was coming. When they stopped calling it Pudding-bag-lane, it became Capel Court.

After the fire, I walked down to Market Strand, near where I used to deal; there was still a bad smell of it in the air. I had a word with the firemen, but they seemed to think it was none of my business. Before they had the road, the women were always out there in their white aprons, forever sweeping with their brushes all day, even those five steps down to the harbour, as if their life depended on it. Come high water, the sand and weed were all back again.

About that time, I got a summons from the council to appear at the Town Hall for arrears in the Poor Rates. Ten shillings they said. I knew Mr Armour by then, and used to help him move furniture in his shop in Fore Street. When I showed him the paper, he said, 'What you going to do, Mr Wallis?'

'They'll come and give me hell if I don't pay,' I said.

'Seems clear that St Ives Council thinks you still run your rag-and-bone shop, Alf,' said Mr Armour. 'Leave it with me, I'll take it up with them.'

A foreigner was living over to Zennor then. I see his wife one time in Mr Armour's shop. They say she sang German songs at night. Others would have it that they saw signal lights aflashing from his cottage to U-boats. The Germans were sinking ships; some good men died off Land's End then. When he was out one time, soldiers got in to search his things. Next day, the police come with dogs and read out a paper. Gave him three days to clear out and never live by the sea again. They had it in the paper.

It was fine weather, so I thought I'd walk over to Tregerthen. I knew where some rabbit-holes were, and had a wire or two in my pocket. I pegged a couple over a burrow.

Foxgloves were still in bloom; there was orange and silver lichen everywhere, crusted at the edges. I could see the view he had of those stony fields going down to the sea. The toecaps of my boots were damp with dew, but it soon dried off. I found a pile of ash where he had burnt his writings. They can say cruel things about a man in these parts, true or false. After a while, I looked in the windows. I could see a vase of dead flowers and other bits and pieces. A spider ran across the floor; they soon know. The room was shipshape; everything was clean and tidy. Mr Armour said she did nothing of that sort, he did it all.

I thought then I might step on as far as Zennor, see who I could see, but I told myself not to bother. Seeing the church tower of St Senara, it called to mind that other devil worshipper who had come to live in the parish with a lot of women. The vicar had run out that church door to throw holy water over him. Satan's man paid no mind. He said the vicar was not a real priest and, if the water had been holy, he would have sizzled. The local magistrates sent the police to get him and his women out of the county. You could never know the far end of those things, nor about that mermaid carved there on the end of the pew.

A mermaid came ashore at Padstow, too, and was shot by an arrow a fisherman fired. Dying, she cursed the town, and cast all that sand into the river mouth. It's no wonder they have wrecks there, or that they need more than one lifeboat. In those days it took six horses to haul the gig.

On the way home, I went to look, but there was no rabbit in any of of the snares. It was all furze, gorse and blackthorn there, and I hunched down quiet to watch an adder asleep.

Old Mr Hesp was sitting near Clodgy Point. He called, 'All right, then?'

'Out for a walk,' I said. 'How's your grandson doing now; how's Jim?'

'He's at the war. Is he going to get back at all, so many of those lads dying?' He went quiet, then said, 'Rain before dark.'

I nodded. 'Looks likely.'

If you go and read the names on the war memorial, their faces come back. You see them turn in the doorway of the pub to smile at a friend, and you look further down and that boy's name is there, too. They could just about splice a rope's end and fish when they were killed. Their widows go by with their fatherless children.

Days follow one after the other. One morning a nail went through the sole of Susan's shoe and I found her sitting in the hearth with blood everywhere. Some things she said then had a lot of malice aforethought. A nail goes into her foot and poison starts to flow from that.

Colonel Benson came around Back Road one spring day just after the war. I had to hire a cart to go up to his place in Carbis Bay, for the stuff he said he wanted to sell.

'I built railways in India before the war,' he boasted. 'You were dealing with the dregs there. The lowest of the low, dogs without a shadow.'

I got to Carbis Bay early, and went down by the beach to wait. I could see a Punch-and-Judy show on the sands. The red striped box was facing away from the sea. There was Mr Punch, big red nose, lunging from one side to the other and hitting Judy about the head. It was the usual story – a wife, a baby, a policeman, a judge, a hanging, and then Punch goes to the Devil. Seemed to me that the children were getting a lesson about what life was like ashore.

I knew where the Colonel said his bungalow was. Two sisters had lived there; they would always give me a cup of tea. There were palm trees growing in the garden and great clumps of pampas-grass. Now there was a smell of creosote coming off the fence. All the curtains upstairs were drawn, as if somebody had died there. I could hear a gramophone and I see Colonel Benson in the front room dancing to the music with a glass of whisky. When he saw me, he pointed the way round to the back.

A girl leaned her head out from the verandah and nodded to where the things were in a neat pile. 'My father will be along, Mr Wallis,' she said, going indoors.

Colonel Benson came out when I was looking the stuff over. Most of it was in three tea chests, old books and magazines. The top one was a wormy brown *Twenty*

Thousand Leagues Under the Sea, and there was a broken record of *Orpheus in the Underworld*. There was a rusty birdcage, some pictures (one of him in uniform before he lost his left arm) an old mangle, a venetian blind, and a lawnmower. I could tell it would work after a drop of oil and sharpening. Only thing worth a few pounds was a scarred brass propeller, but it was not very big. All the bowls had holes where the enamel had come off. One bowl was full of onion sets that were sprouting. 'It's not the sort of stuff I deal in at all,' I said. 'I don't want any onion sets.'

'Nor do I, Mr Wallis,' he said.

I put the bowl on the cart.

He had told me he had seen fighting on the Somme, so he had no need for a gas mask now; or for a shell case and rusty bayonets. He had half a dozen German helmets with spikes, *pickelhaubes*, he called them. He said he had shot the men who'd worn them. The box of lead soldiers and two German medals he kept separate, wanting more for those. I said a price for the whole lot, and he said bugger that. He wanted more than I was willing to pay, but I could tell he was keen to be shot of it so I didn't budge.

I didn't waste any time getting it onto the cart. When I went back for the venetian blind, I saw a tortoise going round the lawn. I could see red dragons on a yellow screen in the dim room in front of where he sat.

He called his daughter, Cora, if she was his daughter. She came out wearing a red party hat to offer a plate of fancy cakes. By now, it was clear that both had been drinking. I could smell it on their breath.

She was a big girl. She wore a black dress with a red belt and golden sandals. Her eyes were dark green. The down on her top lip was so dark she had tried to hide it under thick face powder, but you could still see it. The puff had left marks on her shoulder, and she had smeared her lipstick. Her arms were long. When she was not smiling all over her face, she looked sulky, up to mischief, without being sure how far she would go.

To start with, she brought the gramophone out, gave the handle a turn, and put another record on. She had a paper snake squeaker that she blew in my face as the Colonel beat time on his boot with a riding crop. He began to sound a hunting horn and whoop and holler. I had to be the fox he was about to cut the tail off.

She put her hair against my face and began to cram it in my mouth with her finger. I could see him over her shoulder, sitting in the wicker chair with his legs open and waving that big pistol about. I thought I would choke. Men have strangled women for less.

'You want her, too, you dirty little bugger? How much will you pay me now?'

I got out of there fast, as soon as I heard that. I didn't slow up until I was coming into St Ives. Then the sky went dark suddenly and a squally rain began to blow. I come down the hill at a fair old clip, rattle-banging, gulls ascreeching all around. Everywhere shop blinds flap, shutters bang, any loose things go clack-clack as I went rolling down. All that weight behind was like to run me under it. The handcart moved so fast behind that my legs were going like a chicken's at speed. I had to run one wheel against the kerb to slow down on Tregenna Hill. Coming round by the Scala, where the Queen's Hotel stables used to be, the load shifted. The venetian blind, lawnmower, birdcage, and all the helmets flew off. I had onion sets all over the road. I was glad nobody was about.

Now whichever way I went, I had to go up. I could get

along Fore Street, but I did not know how I was going to face the Digey.

There had been a fire aboard my old boat the *Faithful*. Nobody was on her at the time, and they soon got her to rights again. Everybody came by to hear all about it, how it might have started.

How these things start you never know. Same as the painting, which is now as natural as breathing. It is the first thing I want to do, soon as I open my eyes – that, or I walk down by the harbour. It was there I saw the old boy, and I came up behind to see how he painted.

I could tell what he was about, but what he was doing had no life at all.

It was a slack day. I went back into my shop; I had ship paint there somewhere and I looked out an old canvas. I would paint over the scene, and went down the alley and sat on the steps, shaping up to the thing. The train from St Erth came steaming round the hillside; the lights were on under the battlements of the Tregenna Castle in the sun above the trees. Gulls were ascreeching, slick and plump. Nothing I did could I get right, so I went back in the shop the better to see with my inner eye. There are things to do with your eyes open and others that you shut them tight to see. I kept at it until Susan came in and asked what I was doing. When she saw what it was, she began to laugh. It was a sound that cut clean through me. I put any idea of painting out of my mind.

Susan was the only mother I can say I knew. There was a time during the day she would set aside to cry for her dead children. When I heard her, I used to hope she was shedding a few tears for mine, too.

Her picture on the wall is enough now. She had that done in a studio in Penzance. I was trying to make it out one night

57

when I saw her head tilt over slow to one side. She was asleep. I couldn't think I ever saw her do that before. I was so amazed, I had to go and put my finger on the pulse in her neck. It was a false alarm; she woke with a start and leaned over to look at my watch. 'Getting late,' she said tutting. I knew she would go when I see her coming up the stairs with the candle. Her face in the shadow did look cut out with a hatchet. She was slow. I knew she was sickening for something. Some of those hymns she knew by heart, she was forgetting now.

The next day it was hot, so the door was open. Soon as I came in, I saw her lying on the floor – one foot turned that way, the other this. She was an awkward handful to get up that staircase. Her skin was cold, and Mrs Peters was afraid she'd gone.

Later, I took up a pail of warm water and washed her face and neck. 'You want me to do the rest of you before the doctor comes?'

'No.'

'Not your legs and feet?'

'No.'

'You want I get Mrs Peters in to do it?'

'I don't want anybody in here touching me. Our Jessie will do that when she comes round.'

When Doctor Mathews came, he put a bandage on the cut she had on her forehead. Susan had her eyes open and was scowling at a blue sky.

'No, there is nothing a hospital can do. She is as well-off here, with her family, as anywhere,' he said when he came down. 'She was asking after Jessie and her sons. I think she knows.'

'Knows that she's going to die; is that it, then?'

'I can't say when. She could pass on this afternoon, or be with you still in three months' time.'

I was by the window. Two women rode by on bicycles; one held her hat with one hand, the other rang her bell and laughed as they went down the Digey.

That night I didn't know what to do for the best, but I got into bed beside her. Well, I was stiff for the first time in years, and I got my hand up her nightdress because there was nothing she could do about it. She took a deep breath, then began to hoo hoo like an owl. It was a fearsome sound I had never heard her make before. I got the idea that she was about to die, and that if I went to sleep there I would wake up and find her icy cold. I went off downstairs, and tried to sleep on the couch while listening for any sound upstairs.

It was a grey morning, but I felt we would see a change around noon. I poked the fire and put the kettle on. The lid soon rose and bubbles began to break around the rim. I had a cloth to hand and got it off before it boiled over.

After I made the tea, I poured a cup and took it up. Her eyes were closed. I did not want to, but I tried to feel her heart. At first, I thought it had stopped, then suddenly her eyes opened. I lifted her up to take a sip of tea. She took one, then shook her head.

I pulled the sheet up under her chin; she closed her eyes and set her lips. I could tell she had made up her mind she was not going to speak to me again.

Her children had always clung to her. When they were young, one or other of them was always in her bed with her. After Albert's bread shop went bust she set him up again. He would not feel a bruise if she could help it. It was the same with all of them. Jacob left with seven children to feed and look after when his wife died never wanted for a thing. Where did those children come? To live with us at Bethesda

Hill, all of them. Who was I to stop them swarming round her deathbed?

When I got back with some shopping one afternoon, it was Albert who opened the door. 'We made tea; it'll be cold by now,' he said.

'Then I'll not have one, will I?'

'Don't ask how she is, will you?'

'I'll go up.'

'She could be dead.'

'You'd tell me if she'd gone.'

Even as I went upstairs, I must have been thinking about that chest where we kept the forty-pound in gold and five-pound in silver. I heard them getting their things together to go, then Jessie called up to tell her mother that she would be in first thing tomorrow. I sat on the top step waiting for the door to shut below, then went into the bedroom.

Susan had got the pillow over her face somehow. I took it off quick, or what would those Wards think?

I shook her, but I knew she was gone for this world. First thing I did was to go through the chest to find the money. Every penny we had put by had gone. I don't care which of them took it, but what they did was cruel. I was at their weddings, at the baptisms of their children; their sons and daughters used to climb on my knee to beg for stories. I did my best to be a good father to them when they would let me. I may not have done it, but I tried. I was too old to work steady any more; they had set me on course for the workhouse. What they did between them was to rob me of a safe old age. Now I'm in danger all the days I draw breath. I live in fear of my body failing, of the hospital and the workhouse.

I went down to the privy; I could hardly see my way for tears, but the few pounds I had held back were hidden there.

They had not got their hands on that. It was all I had left, aside from what I had in the Post Office and my pension.

I was thankful that the doctor's bill would not amount to much.

I could hear the midwife from the Salvation Army mumbling on; I didn't know whether she was praying or not. When she left, candles were burning head and foot, and she had put flowers from her garden along the head of the bed.

I held my knees, leaning over to see how Susan was doing. There was a pimple on her cheek, which she could never abide in life. Her bony nose was straight up to the ceiling, hair tight in a hard bun. The woman had washed her, but had not brushed her nails. I took out my penknife and scraped the dirt out. She had tried to cross her hands; they were grey as old lard, one fist was clenched so tight I could not get it open to see if she had a grip on anything in there. That hand had a green marble tint. I could see the plugs in her nose and mouth; her lips were blue, and there was a cloth under her chin hiding her long ears. She was not alive, yet she was not wholly dead. I talked to her awhile and read some psalms she liked. Sometimes I would think I saw her draw breath, but any sort of a twitch, and I would have seen it; there was none. It does not often cross your mind, but the hour does come.

There were flies in the room already, so I hung fly-paper up and opened the window a crack. I sat fanning her face until I heard no more humming. I thought I was brave, Mother, when I took the sheet off and lifted her shift to see what her body looked like that I had lived with all these years. Her feet were tied with footbands and going blue, as if I had beaten them about with a belaying-pin. There had been salty juices there one time, under hair blue-black as a mussel, but never in all the time I knew her. Jacob Ward had the benefit of that, if he ever saw it. Those hairs were strong now as the threads that bind a mussel to the rocks, but her nether lips were wrinkled; there was a brown wart under the grey hairs. No child of mine came out of that hole had lived. Her thighs had shrunk, and her bosoms were grisly paps, suckled flat and lying on her, dry as parchment.

'There were too many of you: the children's mother, the Susan at the heart of the Salvation Army, and the Susan who could talk to the neighbours, if need be,' I said. 'Any time you had left over for me grew less and less. I can't even tell you what it was I wanted. Nor do I want to now, now that you've gone. I was not looking for you, you found me. Did we lie to each other all the time?'

What the Book of Genesis says is that He will put enmity between thee and the woman, and between thy seed and her seed; it shall bruise thy head, and thou shalt bruise his heel.

I lost my temper. She could not answer back now. I had a shock to find myself, working my elbows and crying 'Cock-a-doodle-doo!' as I did a hop and skip around the bed. I was that rooster when he killed Mrs Lander's cockerel.

What brought me up short was that she let one drop suddenly! God Almighty, that fart spread in the room with such an awful stench it drove me out! I did not dare go back, and sat listening all night to every sound.

She was someone I knew, but had become someone I did not want to touch. I guess it was then, that first day, I saw signs she'd turn into Duty Mighty.

I was glad enough to pay the cost of the coffin. All I wanted was to have her out of the house. My heart felt lighter when they got her downstairs and screwed down the lid. I sat quiet as they went about doing things. All the Wards were there, had to be, but I did not want them in. Jessie was crying. I sat, not knowing what to do. I was never deader in my life; all the darkness came inside suddenly, and I sank under it. I had lost my bearings, see. What I thought I was used to, I wasn't.

The Salvation Army was promoting her to Glory. The Major praised her bravery, with all her faults and failings. I said nothing, knowing only how selfish she could be, and how I had to live with her stinting her touch.

'We don't see a lot of you at meetings, these days, Alfred,' the Major said. I was to put down my burden. For I knew where to come if I stood in need of comfort. All I could find to say was that I would try, but I knew I would have my hands full doing pictures. 'I keep to the Bible; that is my chart to Heaven,' I said. 'Though I have to use a magnifying glass to see it, these days.'

They did not have far to carry the coffin – though it was steep, I admit – and I could see that the going was heavy by the time we got up to the chapel.

After they had gone, I went looking at graves, trying to put faces to the names I could remember. A funeral will always humble. Our life span is longer than an eighty-ton whale, for it will die at twenty-four. When any of us goes, it brings it all together, the fear, the loneliness, and lets you know that nobody in this world can console you.

The gravediggers went by, finished for the day, a grunt and a touch of their caps. Their footsteps faded away along the path.

Those hard colours of the sunset can be cruel. They made me think about what she got from God that I could never give her.

'Is she going to get a stone?' Jessie asked.

'How am I to do it? I paid for the coffin. You lot got all the money. Ask Albert about that.'

★

63

I went through the shirt box where she kept her papers, found her birth certificate and the children's. Folded inside her marriage lines to Jacob Ward was the locket she wore when I first met her that opened to show her and Jacob as they used to be. There was a picture of her mother, the one I had seen before. The other photograph was of a woman I did not know, in a nurse's uniform. She had one foot on the running-board of a war ambulance. I found a hairbrush I had bought Susan; she had never used it at all. The surprise was that she had not given it away to Jessie or Emily.

I took her tunic and black straw hat and tambourine back to the Salvation Army barracks. I said I'd put money by from my pension same as usual during Self-Denial Week.

Come home again, I folded the mattress over at the foot of the bed. I was not going to sleep there ever more.

'You were never a true soldier, Alfred,' I heard her say. 'You were too wayward and slippery; real zeal and enthusiasm were missing. You never had the soul of an Apostle.'

Sometimes I feel her close, can still hear her breathing. What it is, a body leaves a house but never goes. On her hands and knees at the step she was some days, shooting a glance up to let me pass. If I drift off, I hear her knitting-needles late at night, nor is that the worst. You'd think she had spent enough years on this earth. There's nothing you can do against their softness, unless you kill them. That softness at bottom is hard as rock. They bring a power against you. What you want most undoes you, turns and strikes you like a serpent. Oh yes, there were things we disagreed about. You'd never hear her say a stranger was coming if there was a sootflake fluttering on the fire bars.

How I tried first to pacify her, I painted her larger than life on the wardrobe door. She was in her black Army uniform. I

64

could not get her to breathe; all I could hear was the clatter of the hangers as she looked for her Sunday dress. The one she had on the day she had flowers and a torn umbrella somebody had lent her. We were hot that day, parched, slaking our thirst together at a public fountain. I can see my hand as I give her the brimming iron cup, the air golden-copper and our throats and shoes caked with dust.

I never go upstairs now at night. Sometimes I hang up washing in the room by day. I put my ear to the door before I go in, in case she's waiting.

How could it be any other way? I could not get that missing money off my mind. It made me see red. I went in there trembling in a rage. Seeing her there, she seemed to be standing by the wardrobe. She used to keep a doll in there she had made for Ellen Jane; I never knew why, only that I hated the thing, and she had set her face against speaking of it when I asked her. Just as she never cared for the magpie, and we had to disagree about that. So I painted a noose around her neck, and said to myself that she was a black-hearted bitch.

'Well, say it now,' I kept on, 'which of them was it, which of your litter got into our chest and took the money? You were in the room. Did you see them do it, and turn a blind eye? You did that because they were your own flesh and blood, and you had one foot in the grave and would never leave that bed.'

Any Ward comes in here now with food, I throw it out, for I know it's poisoned.

Most afternoons I go to Fore Street to chat with Mr Armour, and I call in on Mr Edwards, the watchmaker next door. When tall men grow old they will always stoop; that's how Mr Edwards had become. One of his prize clocks was a white marble archway, a pair of columns each side with the pendulum hung between. There was a lion on top. Sometimes they sent for him to Penzance or Bodmin to fix a clock, or to a church where there was one losing time or stopped. He'd come down from a tower as dirty as a chimney-sweep's boy. I go every week with my gold watch for him to wind. There's an art to winding one of those. I feel calm in his shop, all those clocks passing time away, slow and easy.

'To find out one's longitude at sea, you have to know the time aboard,' Mr Edwards said. 'If a navigator has that, and knows the time at any fixed longitude, he can convert the time difference on the chart. Our earth goes round every twenty-four hours, a full 360° – so one hour will mark one twenty-fourth of a spin, or 15°. The difference of each hour between ship and a known longitude marks a move of 15° of longitude, east or west. That is why, each day at noon, a navigator sets the ship's clock and, after checking the home-port clock, can work out the difference between them into 15° of longitude.'

'You lost me, Mr Edwards,' I said. 'I would always steer by the North Star. Or how we found our way about the sea was by the log, that piece of wood we towed at the end of a line. It had the knots tied in it that would tell the speed of the ship.'

'Without a clock any captain will get lost,' he said.

He showed me a picture of a watch in a magazine.

'John Harrison's H–4 is a national treasure, Mr Wallis. He made it in 1759, and if I were to set it going now, it would still work. But that would wreck it, sure enough. No matter what the oil going around wheels and bearings, it suffers a sea change in time; its viscosity dies, turns acid, and ruins the machinery. That carpenter was perhaps the greatest lifesaver of sailors who ever lived, Mr Wallis. You could say he was ahead of his time. H–4 was a masterpiece; none of them would believe it was so accurate at sea.'

I felt – yes, all at sea. I was alone and feeling deep how everything will change. All flat-fish lie on their side. Some lie to the right, others to the left – but being on the sea-bed, they all see with one eye. Their spry start life up top, then, in time, one eye moves out across their nose, never mind the bone in the way. The marvel is that the bone opens to let the eye go to join the other. Then the blind fish sinks to the sea-bed, white underside down. You see them there, grey-to-green with orange speckles.

Mr Edwards knew none of this, busy with his eyepiece over the parts of the clock, his long fingers fast as a conjuror's. 'Time at sea is not what it used to be,' he said. 'Businessmen's timetables are the true masters now. They fix the departure date, they set another for arrival and return, and woebetide any captain is late.'

I don't know why it was it came into my head then to go at painting proper. Mr Edwards said it was a good idea. It might take my mind off things, my bereavement and all.

I said I would do a bit, it would help pass the time, then went next door to buy two paintbrushes. Said I would get the paint from Joe Burrell in the Digey.

Most of the people here are blood relatives. Everything is habit here. You can do only what is usual. A man strikes out on a new tack, and people start to ask who is he, what's he doing?

If I forget Susan on the wardrobe door, I painted this table first, a two-masted ship making between two lighthouses, one in the top right-hand corner, the other to the bottom left. Later, I put in a fishing boat to square things off. Then I painted a sailing ship between two lighthouses on the bellows, or was it on a Quaker Oats box? I found a flat grey stone on the beach one day; it was in tune with my mood, so I painted that. There's a line of mackerel luggers all along the wainscot there, too, and more gigs on the wall under the window.

After that, I got started on doing an earthenware pitcher, pots and jars. You saw a lot of earthenware pitchers with ships in Devon in the old days.

Mr Armour sells antiques, stuff from all over the world. He has it all: tables, chairs, wardrobes, swords, muskets, ship's compasses, Dresden china, dolls, marbles, a spear he got from the battle at Rorke's Drift. I got to look in a kaleidoscope there. He was telling me that the painter William Turner was in St Ives once, and how I would take him for a seafarer, if I met him, especially in his later years. He had a picture of his fighting *Téméraire*.

I said that people painting ships always made them look bigger than they were.

He said, 'Captain Harvey was in command of her at Trafalgar and making such headway that Nelson hailed him with the horn: "I'll thank you, Captain Harvey, to keep in your proper station." '

Mr Armour can make you feel you are there, in the thick of things. It was Trafalgar all morning while we drank our tea. How the *Victory* came on those last yards, her steering wheel broke and her rigging and sails shot to bits. How a splinter tore the buckle off Hardy's shoe as he strode about the deck with Nelson. Even then, the dear Lord was sure he would not live to see the day out. They were aft of the *Bucentoure*, and gave her a larboard broadside astern, killing and wounding four hundred of the French. Coming after, the rest of the squadron ran into the fight. They were so tight up to the enemy that their guns scraped their hulls. You could not make yourself heard for the thunder. In the cockpit, men fell over bodies in the smoke; the boards were awash with blood; a shambles, a chaplain said. When Nelson was hit, three marines got him below. He had put a handkerchief over his face, so that his men did not twig. He could feel nothing below his waist. He knew the shot had broken his backbone. The battle raged on, all the while he was dying, which he did at half-past four. By then, fourteen of the French had struck their colours and victory was assured.

I wanted to stop Mr Armour, but he had tears in his eyes by then. No sun, no moon, no stars, and the Fleet lost in storms for four days while our dear Lord's corpse spun side to side in a cask of spirit as the *Neptune* towed the *Victory* to Gibraltar for repairs. Going on to England, to St Paul's to be buried by the nation. His admirals and captains walked slow and silent with the funeral car to the 'Dead March' from *Saul*. Hardy is there, and forty-eight of the crew of *Victory*.

I suppose he saw I was agitated, for he said, 'Seems to me that's as much a load as the bridge will bear.'

I ran off home quick, my mind awhirling. I set about painting the *Victory*, but left out half of those ninety gun ports so that I could get on with a picture of the hulk I saw as a boy, anchored at Hamoaze under the bridge at Saltash.

You'd see bodies come off the hulks, some were in old boxes, but most were wrapped in a sheet; only a few got buried. Mostly they were going off by train to London for doctors and surgeons to cut up.

It was a wash day; every court and yard had sheets drying. I put on my best suit. I had it written out, ready on a piece of card:

ALFRED WALLIS
BORN AUGUST 18, 1855
THE FALL OF SERVESTERPOOL
NORTH CORNER DEVENPORT
RUSSIAN WAR

I thought of it as a calling card – my certificate of merit I told Mr Baughan as he stood looking at it; he was a younger man then. I had sized him up already, when Susan used to shop there. She had told me of his serious bent. Still, he has to be careful what he says to me. I had seen all those cards in his window and the boxes the groceries came in. What did he do with them? Did he burn them, or throw them away? I was in need of cardboard, any shape, any size would do. He did not ask why I wanted it, and when he did see what I did with it, he smiled and gave a nod. 'Take any one of them you want,' he said. I asked him only that one time. Ever after that, I had no need to go back. He would look some out and leave it outside in the alley with the milk.

He has a fine forehead, and his nose is good and big. We get on. I know he likes me because I always have a story to tell.

What I got now is something to look forward to. I get out of bed, and I know it's there, waiting, all of it. 'I have a goodly number done by now,' I said. 'I can sit smoking my pipe while I call up times past, and they make it easier to reflect on those.'

Sometimes in the spring, if I feel low, I pick primroses for her grave and go there to sit a bit. We had been companionable most times, as regular as a pair of magpies. I can see her sharp and clear come round the New Street corner into Market Jew Street. Our whole life together comes up in a rush. I used to know the exact number of steps it took to get

70

from Penzance Harbour to her front door. It was not till we came here that she would side with the Army against me, but all that was between her and God. Down from Barnoon Cemetery, I could see two women on the beach with their umbrellas up against the drizzle.

What they say about me? Oh, I know what they say. I am another of those lost souls I used to see go about the streets and wonder at. Going back-along the years there was a fishwife whose family had died at sea. She kept on moving. She never stood still except to sell a pilchard out of her basket. All weathers, too, sometimes you'd see her away off out on the moor on a day not fit for a dog. I saw her go out there in a snowstorm that might have buried her (a good way to go, I suppose). No, there she was on the Wharf next morning, same as always. Only way to talk to her was to try to keep up alongside her; snip, snap – the words would come at you over her shoulder, and she had a heavy weight of fish hanging on her back. The other was a man whose name I never knew. He kept his trousers up with a length of clothes-line. The shoes he wore were too small for him; he had cut the seams down the back to get them on. He was always looking at the watch Mr Edwards gave him. He could wind the hands round, but there was nothing else about it that went. He liked to toss up a handful of coins. See which come down heads, which come down tails. Would do that for an hour at a time.

I am alone now, as they used to be. One day they were not there, nor did they pass by the next, and I was left to ponder their fate.

The other day, I saw something I had never seen before in St Ives, two nuns black as crows telling their beads. I hear strange voices all the time; they go by my window. People come and go all day, children with buckets scrape their spades along to the beach. There are more people now than there used to be when we came here. There are faces in the streets in summer I have never seen before. You have to wait longer in shops to buy what you want. Fishermen's sons and daughters don't stay where they grew up. Women go to swim now and you can see all of them, clear as day. Back-along then, you had to run out of a bathing machine. There were tents first on Porthminster, and then Mr Chard would charge threepence to hire his Pickwick Tents. They have got the name right through pink sticks of rock, and there never used to be those postcards there are for sale now, with views of St Ives. Sometimes they show four pictures in one. To look at those you would never think that storms here turned ships over and killed the crews. Pierrots would come to sing and dance. Gramophones play on beaches where I've seen drowned men's bodies lying stiff as statues.

Some people may look like you and me, but they are from other dark places. I keep away from them, soon as I see those wrongdoers acoming to create havoc. There will be that day of reckoning – so, as you grow older, you can't become less religious. St John's visions are as true today as when he wrote them down.

I have a bird's-eye view already to see how the land lies. Houses go up or go down a hillside, with the arm of Smeaton's pier pointing down. All around is the sea, and what that is, is the same and ever changing. Go down the rocks and find a pool, it is not the same as when the tide went out last. Some creatures have gone, others come in their place, and yet you feel they are your very own, washed home again. You can be young in it, and hold dear all those mysteries you will never fathom. What is kelp about, and why? How do starfish get such a grip on a mussel as to open it up that tiny bit to squirt their juice in, then shift their stomach inside to eat out the flesh?

I sit for hours looking down into rockpools. Why does a grown man do that? Because I got more time now to see what I missed as a child. Anyway, time doesn't matter in there at all, the bladderwrack swinging to and fro around Clodgy. You can find enough big mussels to make soup with. I get those. No matter how big or rough the surf, it can never wash away a bed of mussels.

It's the rockpools I marvel at, though, places where the sea shows off a few of its wonders: prawns you can see through, they are so faint, urchins, anemones, and sea slugs hanging sheets of eggs. It's all muscle in there, see, on a par with the labours of Hercules. It takes a lot of effort for any creature to stay put when the waves come pounding back. The piddocks eat away at the granite for a million years, but they bring a cliff down. They eat nothing else but rock. Ship-worms do it faster to any wood they find, and you wish they didn't; they eat their way through whole navies.

At first, I thought it was the sea, but it came too regular for that. I opened the window, afraid that the noise was in my own head. When I did make it out, I wondered why a steam engine was at work on the Island. I had a mug of tea and set off to see what was going on. Turned out there was a fair; a lot of here-today-and-gone-tomorrow people were jostling me along the street.

I was going through Upalong. The marmoset on the wall held a round pink hat, with her tail hooked round a prop. Nine inches long, she had black fur with a red-brown streak in the middle of her back. She saw me coming along, black eyes adarting this way and that as she ate caterpillars off the nasturtiums. Soon as I came up, she leaped off the wall and ran up my trouser leg until she got on my shoulder. There, she sat twittering with a soft clicking noise in my ear. 'She's taken to you, Mister,' said the organ-grinder.

'Animals will do that.'

He had a bowler hat on, same as me, but I could tell he had been a seaman. His skin was smooth and brown as cocoa with a dash of milk. He had only one shoe on; the other was a wooden leg stuck out from a cut-off pair of canvas pants. 'I'm not so handy up the rigging any more,' he said with a smile.

The marmoset left my shoulder for the organ.

'I got her in Bélem, as a baby,' he said, his monkey running to grab a handful of peanuts from a dish.

'I heard the steam engines,' I said, nodding up at the fair.

'It's the first day. Better tomorrow, and the weekend.'

'You're with them?'

'No. I travel alone, but if there's a fair I can make a few pence. This one is too near the end of the world for my liking.' He filled his pipe. 'I used to be at sea, like you.'

'How did you know I was a sailor?'

'By the easy way you rolled along down that street. There's no mistaking that walk.'

He seemed jolly enough; he had been through a few scrapes at sea and seen some dark times.

'Life is mostly uphill,' he said. 'I was just a boy; a bos'n plied me with hot liquor and I was shanghaied. I woke up with a terrible headache. If I made any kind of murmur, I was in chains again. Out of the frying pan into the fire, as they say.'

'I'm Alfred Wallis,' I said.

'They call me Cairo,' he said. 'That's where I come from.'

'In Egypt?'

'No, America. Near New Orleans, where I was shipped out.'

A clown with an umbrella ran out of the fair. His big black shoes flopped from side to side going along. He was spinning a plate on a wand and he had a flower in his buttonhole that squirted water to make the girls scream.

I asked Cairo if he fancied to drink a pot of tea. He took out a picture of his wife to show. He said she had been the daughter of a slave.

'Will my organ be safe outside? There are kids, you know, and it's my only livelihood.'

'There's room for it in the passageway.'

As we went along together, he told how a storm had swept his ship past Gibraltar. They missed the dockyard there and had to hove-to at Tangiers for repairs before they dared go out into the Atlantic. It was one trip he did not care to recall. 'You break your back straining over an oar to get a handful of oranges, but you never step ashore; the sea runs too strong against you. And there they are – the trees are thick with them hanging bright, so full of juice your jaws ache.' He laughed. 'Never mind what I say, Mr Wallis, I expect I hope I'll sign on again.'

'It's number three, the one with the green door,' I said. 'You go along there while I get some milk.'

You may wonder at that, but nobody who could put himself in a yarn the way he did was going to run off with any of my goods. When I came in the door, he was going up close to look at the paintings.

'My, my, but you put some work in here, Mr Wallis,' he said. 'I never in all my life saw the like of this.'

I felt proud to hear that tone in his voice. I gave him a cut off my tobacco plug. He went around looking awhile, smoking, and stopping only to ask a question now and then.

Being a storytelling man, though, no sooner did he finish one tale than he would launch into another.

'We were bound for the Azores when the storm struck,' he said. 'In all the hurly-burly of a heavy gale, the key of the steerage door was lost. Naturally, we said it must have washed overboard. Then all kinds of things began to vanish: marlinspikes, cold chisels. Well, you must know as well as I do that nothing can get out of place on a ship. So it was only reasonable to think that they were gone over the side. It was so many oddments, though. Every man was a suspect, every man guilty in his brother's eyes. You will know how we felt – living cheek by jowl with some guy whose face was set against the rest out of malice and devilment. Then food went from the pantry, even though the steward locked it every night and gave the key to the captain. One morning the steward found the cupboard bare, and we were all on hard tack. It was the captain who tumbled when he tried the pantry key in the steerage door. The locks were the same. To foil the thief, he put a padlock on the pantry door.

'That didn't stop it all. Whoever it was took to cutting ropes in the rigging, and put all our lives at risk.'

'Did you ever find him out?'

'He gave himself away. Captain Auerbach was selling boots and clothing out of the slop-cask when the man went up bold as brass with a pair of shoes he said were now too small for him. He asked whether Auerbach would swap him another pair? The captain obliged. Then, stowing gear away in the cask again, the captain felt something shift in one of the shoes. He put his hand in and it was the key of the steerage door, missing then for a year.

'Auerbach played dumb. Putting a pair of darbies in his pocket, he had the culprit in his cabin. Showing him the key, the captain wanted to know how it got in his shoe. The man

76

smiled, and was told to wipe that look off his face. He set about answering back, making a raging denial, laying it on others. The captain would stand for none of that.

'At last, the man got nasty, and Auerbach hit him squarely with his fist, locking the darbies on him. He put the barrel of a pistol in his mouth, and said: "If you know any prayers, now's the time!" The man's face was yellow, and he threw up a mess of slop on the deck.

'It was just such a knockout that started the trouble in the first place. Auerbach had found fault with that guy earlier in the trip, and he had set about drinking himself into a one-man mutiny. Soon as the captain came on deck, he began to tongue-lash him, boasting that Auerbach did not have the guts to face him, man to man. "I'll fight any three officers you name," he crowed. His mouth was still open when Auerbach hit him. It didn't close until he fell down the stairway into a heap on the steerage floor.

'Auerbach was no angel; he could only blame himself, for that devil was of his own creation. He would rant at the crew in German, and any man who did not hear or understand his orders could expect a smack in the mouth. Apart from a word or two, it went in one of my ears and out the other. All a man could go by was the high colour of his cheeks, or the look in his eyes the instant before he hit him. Then he knew to step out of the way.

'Auerbach ordered two of us to tie the man and haul him up the mizzen stay. You will know that pain, how the skin comes off your ankles after swinging there an hour, let alone two, which was the time he hung. After that, he could go about his duties by day, but was under lock and key at night. All the crew must shun him, say not a word, until we could drop him in our next port of call.'

Men are not of the same stamp, I said, the sea brings out

77

only what you have in you, whatever that is. A mean man becomes meaner, a shirker, an idler who will do only as much as he has to do to get by. Most men sing, but there are some who go about as if the end of the world was nigh, silent and dark. Others will go at life with the ferocity of a rat to suck the yolk out of an egg. 'Retribution is God's work, not ours,' I said.

When he left I could hear his barrel-organ down by the harbour. I thought about him in the night, on the road somewhere.

I never mind being alone but, with Cairo gone, I was restless; I tried to paint but nothing came right. I was wasting cardboard, and the paint cost money. Rain was streaming off the roof, rattling down from the gutter in the pipes. I fell asleep on the couch and had a dream.

In the dream, I had swum out to sea, never to come back. I was far enough out to feel alone, and could not see the land. As I was about to roll over and float awhile, I felt hands catch at me. A drowning person had come up from some wreck and was fighting to reach the air. I came face to face with a woman who might have pulled me under. Only her nose was above the water; her eyes were two black pits. When they opened, I heard her cry. 'I have to get you out of this,' I said. She closed her eyes, and I thought I heard her say, 'Be gentle, won't you?'

I got her head between my hands and, towing her behind, began to kick out for land. Soon as I heard the breakers, I felt her sink again, and I woke up with tears streaming down my face. She was Kezia, and that captain's wife; she was Alice Fincher, Susan as a girl and my lost mother too.

What Mrs Phillips said, who had watched me go by with Cairo, was that she had never before seen a Negro in the flesh; it was true that they were as black as the Ace of Spades.

Her cat's kittens were frisking all around her on the doorstep.

'Well, now, I thought his skin was more cocoa coloured,' I said.

To look at that dog now you'd think it was asleep, but I keep the other side of the street, ready to kick when he strikes. I been standing here I don't know how long, sunk in all that stuff set out on the front: watering-cans, baskets, ropes, rolls of wire mesh, boxes of nails, baskets, and bundles of wood for fire lighting. I can't seem to get my bearings. When I come to my senses, I am biting the stem of the pipe. So I feel in my jacket pocket to find the matches and take them out. That cost an effort, and I lost my puff.

Came to me then where I was bound. I get my Old-Age Pension now, and I was going to the post office to collect it, the clerk thumping every stamp St Ives, St Ives. I can remember the money I had there, after Susan died, but I did not want to think about that.

When Reuben Sadd first came knocking, he said Mr Hollow had sent him. I liked him on sight, an old greybeard, and he began to visit here often. We read the Bible together, and I'd play the melodion while we let rip on some grand old hymns.

'Somebody said once that religion is the opium of the people,' he told me.

What did that man mean by that?

'If I understand it right, religion is what the squires and parsons put us to sleep with, so that we dream instead of doing something about those evils in the world that need changing now.'

'Is that how you see it, Reuben?'

'I can only say that I am godfearing when I look into His face.'

'See Him, do you, Reuben. He appears to you?'

'Except those nights when the soul is dark; then I fall to thinking about Lenin's Red Flag and what is happening in Russia. There is a civil war going on there, a lot of people dying – now they are dropping like flies of hunger. It is a famine as bad as those we read about in the Bible.'

'You know more about that than I do, Reuben.'

'We have to find it in our hearts to help those people, Mr Wallis. All they want is happiness for mankind. Both of us know no ship can sail without a crew; nor can any one man build a bridge alone. Nor do you have to love or like the men you sail with, only to know that without them you would die.'

So he could see nothing wrong with killing the Tsar, his wife and children, or men and women striding about with hammers and sickles. He did not want to foul anchors with me over that, he said. 'These people are living the shape of things to come. In the end, it will be the same for us, when you and I go side by side beside the Galilee, those fishes shining and multiplying, as we eat that bread from heaven.'

Reuben said we had to struggle along as best we could with what we think we know. 'We have seen the best of it; I can't look forward any more, ever. I am bound for that good place soon, Alf.'

'You aim to go, then?'

'I am worn out, having to stand on guard all the time. Life is always a struggle, as we both know. You have to fight so hard for everything, even meaning.'

There, he had done it again. Left me stranded, lost altogether.

He stood up. 'Who will mourn us when we die, Alf?'

I went up the road with him. 'Will you come tomorrow?'
'Where else would I go?'

I turned at the corner as he began to climb the hill. The sea was breaking white in the moonlight. I held my watch up and could see, clear as day, that it was three o'clock.

I saw him two days later, he was a ten-year-old coming along the Wharf, hopping over pools the rain had left, and he came the next night.

After we ate the stew I made, we sang and talked as usual. I don't think he'd eat anything at all unless I made him. Even then, he will only do it to humour me. Just as I was thinking that, he got up and said, 'I think your food is too rich for my stomach, Alf.'

He went behind into the kitchen and was sick in the pail.

'Are you all right, Reuben?' I called.

He came back and sat down again. Big drops of sweat fell off his forehead as he leaned over the table with his hands between his knees. He was right as rain, he said, and I got him to promise to come again on the Friday as he left. When he didn't come, I thought – well, maybe tomorrow.

There was no sign then of him at all, so I went round to the house where I knew he lodged. It was my first time there. The landlady had a man's socks on and a pair of plimsolls. When we got up to his room, the door was locked. No answer came to our knocking; his landlady was saying she hadn't heard him go out. I broke my knife to get the door open.

On coming in we found him dead. He had no shirt or shoes on. His back was towards the door and was covered in blood. I went round to see his face; I could not believe he was dead. He had one of his braces over his shoulder; the other was in the crook of his elbow, as if he had been trying to get it on when he fell. The landlady said the chair was not where it usually stood, against the wall. He had sat, or knelt there, to hold it, which seemed likely from the way he lay. The whip on the chair was stained, and there were flecks of blood on the window-pane. His hairless chest was covered with a big tattoo, the serpent coming down the tree in Eden, the apple ready in its mouth for a naked Eve, while Adam was trying to look the other way. Flying above, there was a woman who could have been the Virgin Mary had she not held a Union Jack. Only a mariner could have such a thing on his body, yet he had never said he was at sea. The strangest thing was that he had a red skullcap on his head, which I felt I had to take off and put in my pocket.

'You are white as a sheet, Mr Wallis,' said Mrs Gulyas. 'We better have a glass of whisky. Mr Sadd keeps a bottle in that cupboard by the bed.'

'A bottle?'

She took the whisky out. 'He has no need for it now,' she said, filling a glass.

I said no, shaking my head; my gaze would not leave his back and that brutal whip on the chair. I knew what the scourge was; I had seen one before. It was an old navy cat-o'-nine tails. They had killed men with those.

I don't know why, but I could not get Yankee off my mind. We were all sure-footed at sea. I could see Yankee coming back drunk, and that night when he did not come at all. None of us saw him then or the next day. The light was failing when Jack tied a grappling-hook to a line and began to haul it, hoping it might snag on his clothes. The water was not deep there. I had my hand on Jack's shoulder when I felt him tense up. The hook had snagged Yankee's waistcoat; fumbling to button it, as usual he had left most of it gaping. We had to haul him up, arms and legs awry, water gushing out of every pocket. His eyes were open with a look of surprise, so was his mouth, and in the winter light his face shone green. Reuben had something of the same look, with his fly buttons undone.

Mrs Gulyas said the drink was not the only thing. Mr Sadd had a tart. She came over on the Penzance train, or by bus sometimes, and went off again the next day. She had been with Reuben the night before.

'Do you know her name?'

'I got better things to do. I let her in. Who she was, or what he got up to with her, was none of my business, if he paid the rent. Who can tell what they do in Penzance? They do it all there. Sailors come ashore; they've not seen a woman in months, and they want a frolic, and they know where to go. Not every house is pious in that town, even if they like to make out they are.'

There was a piece of paper rolled into a bloodstained ball under the window. I picked it up and smoothed it out. It was a drawing. Reuben had tried hard to make sure you could tell that the kneeling man was Christ. You knew the matchstick men scourging him were Roman soldiers because of their helmets. Christ had a message coming out of his mouth; it said, 'Harder; do it harder!' It was as if Reuben never spoke a word to that woman. She had come, knowing full well what he wanted, and he would hold up the drawing while she lay that cruel thing across his back.

Had she been there when he died? Where could she go if it was the middle of the night? Did she lie there in the room with him, or did she run out and walk St Ives until first light and the early train? Ever after that, I could imagine her, if I came down Barnoon Hill, going through Tregenna Place and along The Terrace.

The landlady said Mr Sadd had taken some of his clothes out yesterday and made a fire of them in the garden. She had to tell him about the smell, and he said they would soon burn. 'I know I'm going to have to get an exorcist in,' she said, with a shudder. 'I can feel that already.'

I stared at the religious pictures on the wall; they showed Christ with his head all bloody from the crown of thorns. In another, he had the big weight of the cross on his back. There was one of a painting Reuben had torn from a magazine. It was so dark it came into my soul. In it, Jesus hung like a piece of bad green meat on a bent cross. That scourging had torn pits in his flesh. His mother was by the cross, with St John the Evangelist holding her up while she wrung her hands. On the other side stood St John the Baptist with a Bible, pointing a long finger at Christ.

What was a painting of mine doing among such things? Reuben had liked it, so I gave it to him. It was Nelson's *Victory*. I did not want people to see it among all that Catholic stuff. I got it down, folded it in a newspaper, and put it in my coat.

The smell in the room now came from the gasworks, and it was bad. I shut the window and bolted it. 'You better go get a doctor,' I said. 'Find a policeman, too, because there's nothing right about this.'

I had the same feeling of, why did he do that awful thing? Same as the day we found Mr Lott hanging from the spar at first light, and all that sea that he could have quietly gone into without a murmur. Not strangling up there for us to find him and have a job to get him down. Looking at Reuben there, dead, and keeping all his secrets, all I could think of were those lines in the scriptures that put you outside of the mystery.

You cannot tell a policeman this when he asks. It was also true that I was trying to deny Reuben. I did not want to admit that he was ever a near friend of mine. I did not like to do that, but I was afraid where it all might lead.

'Do you know where Mr Sadd was from?'

I shook my head, thinking then that for all the time we had spent together, I knew nothing about him.

'He was not a local man. We don't even know that he was Cornish. He did not only sing hymns, Mr Wallis. Mrs Gulyas says that he brought a low woman here some nights. His back, now, well I don't think any man has the fortitude to inflict those wounds on himself, so it seems likely that she was here to flog him last night. Mrs Gulyas says she was here, so she is the prime suspect; but what sort of a woman can do that to a man? I don't believe Mrs Gulyas heard no sound, that he could bite his lip through that and never cry out.

I can say nothing. I'm not clever enough to fathom it, nor will the police do much to find it all out. 'Reuben was my friend,' I said. 'This has come very hard. Can I go home now?'

There was an ambulance outside when I got downstairs. A young policeman, I did not know him, had his arm out to caution half the street, who were there to have a look. I heard him tell them to go home, that there was nothing to see. By the time I reached the end of the street and stood to look back, two men had come out with Reuben wrapped in a sheet and lashed to a stretcher.

I was afraid they'd think I had poisoned him, but I heard nothing more. Then Mr Hollow and I buried him in the paupers' end of Barnoon.

I felt I had to stop by Susan's grave coming back, to have a few words with her about Reuben. To tell her I had thought him a saintly man who was too good for this world, but Mr

Hollow was there, so I took him home with me and made some tea.

'I think Reuben Sadd would have felt better if we'd stitched him in a hammock and sunk him with a length of chain,' said Mr Hollow, looking at his watch.

'I could not believe the mess his back was in,' I said. 'Did you ever see the tattoo on his chest?' I said it was no quick dagger in a rose. He had not been idle in some port and one of his mates said he knew of a parlour, where they went after a few drinks. Nor was it one of those things you get trying to prove your mettle as a lad, when they do a dirty drawing on your skin with gunpowder and set fire to it. You would dock at Portsmouth with a picture you could not show your mother. I told him about the straps I had seen on the bed, which she could buckle to spreadeagle Reuben for punishment. 'It's all to do with old navy times,' I said.

'I don't know why I had a sense that he had come ashore after a life at sea,' said Mr Hollow. 'That's why I sent him to you.'

'I was always glad you did that,' I said. 'We spent some grand times together.'

'We're all pilgrims, Mr Wallis, and you get wherever it is we're going, one way or another. There are some that might say that Reuben was sick. I am not one of those. I say, God relented in good time and let him die.'

Everybody wanted it swept under the carpet, soon as you like. Reuben was a poor stranger; he had died in the last place where they would want to raise too much dust.

'The quicker they buried him the better,' Mr Hollow said. 'They got the doctor to sign a death certificate to save the expense of an autopsy. An autopsy might have found signs of foul play. No, they never tried to look any further.'

'Are we going to?' I asked.

'That's the saddest part. I don't see what we can do, either.'

'Maybe if I went and asked around Penzance, I could find that woman he was seeing.'

'Was it her who killed him? That is the only question, so far as I can see it. If she didn't, I don't think she'd know any more than we do, Mr Wallis. We are innocents in such an affair, and I see no sense in dabbling in it. It's a puzzle neither you nor I can explain. I bang up against it like a rock, and my mind goes blank. It sinks me. He took us both in, Alfred. It would not have come as a surprise if they had found a hair shirt in there, as well as that evil whip.'

Now I have no company at all. I got nobody coming to look forward to except Mr Hollow. He was the only real friend I had then, until he died.

Children are the least able to cope with that great cruelty with which men treat them. Those in power over them give them men's jobs to do before they have the strength. They say that children must learn, and that's true, but you do not put a child in danger before it can deal with it. Children are sent out into the dark, into places where grown men fear to go.

I was told when I first went to sea that the only reason they had boys aboard was to eat them if they had to take to the boats. Nobody who has ever sobbed himself to sleep as a child can object to what I'm saying.

Some children deal in sniggering grunts, like pigs rooting for acorns, and the ones I came across were doing that. They were all boys, apart from a girl who was with them. She had red hair and was called Kezia. The sleeves of the man's jacket she wore were too long, and she had rolled them up. She held it open at the collar and swayed to and fro flaunting her breasts. I see them first in Porthgwidden there, where some fishermen had beached a basking shark after towing it inshore. The men had cut every useful bit out of it, liver and oil, and left the carcass with its mouth propped open with spikes. The light was going fast as I walked across and found two of the boys had got inside and were cutting at its stomach lining. As I warned them against what they were doing, the others kicked the spikes away so that the jaw fell shut. The Jonahs were screaming in there now, while the others laughed. I got one foot on the lower jawbone and heaved it open to let them out. Ever after that, I was to blame in some way.

The light had almost gone by then. I could barely see the two cormorants on Bamalûz Point preening to dry their feathers. The boy they had buried, and told not to move, lay there in the sand trying to whistle. That sand must have been cold by then. The others had left him, had run off chanting, and he was crying now. The girl shook him, then licked a handkerchief to rub his cheeks where his tears had run through the dirt.

You leave the door wide to let the sun light up the paintings. So I saw their shadows first. Mr Ben gave the door a tap and come walking in. I'd heard painters do that – step into your front room without any by your leave. What was the name they called me – Cézanne? I think what Mr Kit said was something after that. He had a game leg; had the arms of his sweater tied round his neck like a schoolboy and wore plus-fours. They were artists, too, they said, and both did envy the way I handled colours.

'You don't want to use too many of those,' I said. 'And all of them got to belong.'

They were nosing round at all the paintings. 'What's this?

88

A coffin?' Mr Kit gave it a rap and asked what I used the box for.

'I put it on the couch to sleep in,' I muttered. 'It's more of a bunk to keep the draughts out. Some nights I wish it had a lid.'

I told them that, at first, I was going to write my life down for something to do, but I had never been any good with words. I had a logbook I kept once when I was at sea. I burned it, too, when I took to painting. 'All those things I paint are real, you know; they happened,' I said.

'Those are big nails,' said Mr Kit.

'All I had. They hold them there, though.'

I went over to the oven and took out the teapot and said, 'You want a cup? It might be too stewed for your taste.'

I poured three cups, but I see they only took a sip of theirs.

'You've got a snug house here, Mr Wallis,' said Mr Ben.

'Houses – I don't like houses! Give me a ship any day of the week, and you can have all the houses in the world.'

Mr Kit could not get over how big I had made one of the fish in a picture, down dark under the keel. 'That fish is standing for all the fish that ever swum,' I said, 'for all the fish that God ever put in the sea, that's why it's so big and powerful.'

Sometimes the shape of a bit of cardboard will put me in mind of a scene I saw once, and will make it easier to get at it. 'I did this three-master on this calendar because of the shape,' I said. 'See how neatly her spanker fits in that curve. No, I never trim a card, I find my way to arranging what I want to do in there, whatever the shape is.'

'I like that; I like that a lot,' said Mr Ben. 'Very economical.'

'What they laugh at in my paintings, worries me most to get right,' I said. 'Mr Laity is a grocer and general dealer on the Wharf Road. I used to buy my tea from him, and he would come round here and I could never explain to him why that ship was on end. He would say, "Now, Mr Wallis, I never saw any boat go round the quay on end that way." Well, how else do you show it? What I like about cardboard is that it comes in the shapes that fit my guessing. The other thing I fancy doing is to leave the colour of the board as it is, brown, green, or whatever. I use any sort I can lay hands on, I buy yacht paint from Joe Burrell in the Digey, or I thin down ripolene house paint with turpentine.'

Mr Ben said he never knew why they called them ketches. I told him ketch was the stuff we dyed the sail with.

'You seem to have seen quite a bit of the world,' Mr Ben said, looking at a picture of a schooner. He asked what I called it.

'I suppose you can call it the schooner and the moon. That ship is on the other side of the earth, for it is there the moon looks like that. Most places I saw, I went by sea: in Mexico once, then in among fjords, and great icebergs in green water,' I said. 'The frost opened all my finger-ends. I saw a lot of creatures. One thing I never saw in the flesh was a camel, but I did see a donkey with stripes. They were asking a lot of money for that, and I put it in one of my paintings.'

Mr Kit looked at me long and hard enough for me to tell he was serious and said, 'What would your best advice be to a painter, Mr Wallis?'

'My father always said leave something for your master to find fault with, that he can talk about; otherwise you won't hear a word.'

Mr Ben gave me two-and-sixpence for a schooner and lighthouse I had done, and asked right in my ear, 'When were you born, Mr Wallis?'

'At Devonport, during the Crimean War, 18 August 1855, the day Sebastopol fell,' I told him.

'That would make you seventy-three,' said Mr Kit. 'How long have you been painting?'

'I started six years ago.'

'So late?' Mr Ben seemed surprised, looking round.

'I did it for company,' I said. 'Then old Mr Armour told me I had done a mighty fine job when I showed him some. After that, I just kept on going.'

'Are these all of your work? How many are there?'

'I forget how many I do.'

'A thousand?'

'Could be, could be close on that.'

'You don't have names for your paintings?'

'No, I know what they are – that one hung up I do often. She is the *Belle Adventure* of Brixham at Labrador, Newfoundland, and those are icebergs,' I said. 'I must have been nineteen then. It was a hard trip, but I lived to see Teignmouth again in the autumn.'

When they asked why I put Godrevy so close to the Island, I said it's where I want it to be. 'Unless you go to sea, you can never feel what a lighthouse means,' I said. 'Whenever there's a storm, you will always see a lighthouse in my pictures. There has been a light on Godrevy since 1859. It was built four years after the SS *Nile* ran onto The Stones there. The Irish Steam Company owned her; all sorts of wreckage and women's bodies washed up.'

'You were only a child.'

'That's as maybe, but I know about it.'

I sold Mr Ben a three-master, and Mr Kit wanted a two-master I had done. A car came for them to go. The driver had a bowler hat and sat stiff as a bolt. I got my hand behind my ear to hear what they said. Mr Ben was going on about how amazing it was they had found me. I made him think of Gogol. Who?

Mr Kit looked back. 'How can you say that?'

'Emerson got it wrong, then?'

'You can't still read him? What are we to do about the Admiral?'

'Everything we can that he will allow; nothing that will stop him doing what he wants the way he wants to do it. We must get some of his pictures to Jim Ede.'

Mr Kit came back a few days later and said he would like to see me paint. 'Can I watch? Just say if I'm in the way.'

I shook my head and got on with what I was doing.

He said he felt it was fate that had drawn us together. He had brought me some baccy and newspapers: a *John O' London's Weekly*, a *Daily Herald* and the *News of the World*. I had never read that paper until then. I found out why soon enough.

Mr Kit was still a boy; his natty bow-tie was too old for him. I had never been a boy. He knew the story of Peter Pan, which he told me – I did not ask why. It was one he knew and it passed the time. The boys were all lost, like Peter Pan, who had no mother, and always wanted one. Mr Kit said God had blessed him with the dearest mother in the world. She was from a Cornish family of seafarers, too. After he caught polio at school, they sent him home. He was in great pain. His father was in France, tending the wounded, so his mother took care of him. She had read about an Australian nurse who had been using massage to help patients. So for three years his mother would work hours on his legs to get life back into them. He may limp now, but without her devotion he would not walk at all. After all that, he said, 'Well, I had to get out of bed, Mr

Wallis. I ran sweat to get across that room. It was the only course I had, if I wanted to be the greatest painter in the world.'

'Are you anywhere near?'

'Not by a long chalk, Mr Wallis. All we can do is keep trying, eh? All I can hope is that I will paint pictures one day that will be worthy of her.'

When he stood with his legs apart, you could never tell, unless he took a step, that he had a limp.

Death was always round the corner, he said, and when you least expected it. He had been on the last boat out of Smyrna; a day later, the Turks marched in and murdered everybody.

It was like a bad dream sometimes: he knew the song, yet he never felt he was singing the right notes. He said he wished he could paint sea and ships the way I did, and he tried, but never had the right feel. I told him, if he had spent as many years as I had at sea, he would know about sails, ropes, and the weather.

'What's this heap here on deck?'

'Washed slack, Mr Kit. She is heading for the White Sea, and has to ship all the coal she can carry.'

The other boats were fleeters, I said; they night-fish by the light of acetylene lamps, then head into the East Coast ports early morning to box their codlings, smelts, whiting and haddock in time for the market train. I showed him the painting I had done for Mr Ben. He asked me what I called it, and I said all I knew was that it was some cottages in a wood in St Ives. 'The man is having a bit of a sit-down walking his dog. Mr Ben said he liked the way I was doing the cottages. It was as if I'd scored them on a slate.'

I told him I didn't care for it much. It was nearly always ships. If I did a picture on land, it would have birds or animals. I could not make a good job of shore life, especially a wood: I was a babe in that gloom. You never know who's coming up behind you, and there are owls there, and they are white. I was glad to get away. I had come to a run-down place and asked the old woman for a glass of water. The nettles stood above my head, and she had geese she was fattening up for Christmas. They shit everywhere in the yard, she said and gave one her shoe up its backside. They would get into the house to do it, too. I asked her, was it worth it?

'So we're the same in some respects,' he said. 'I like to think I paint pictures that come out of my own life. And I should imagine you find it as hard to tell lies as I do, Mr Wallis.'

Mr Kit is staying at Meadow Cottage behind Mr Baughan's shop. We get on fine together except I hate it when he calls me Admiral. He showed me a painting he had by Van Gogh, and how do I like it? Oh, well enough except he used too many colours and spoiled his pictures. There was one drawing I liked – three boats drawn up on the sand.

Mr Kit had a map of the world on the wall, with a compass in one corner and a cherub with fat cheeks out to blow a ship in the other. There were some sea pinks, some fresh, and some dead, stuck down one side.

He showed me a painting he had done. He called it 'China Dogs in a St Ives Window.'

'You see, you move Godrevy where you want it, too.' I said. 'You made that stack too high for her size, though.'

In another painting of a window he had done, the sea was dark outside and he had an oil-lamp on the right and that long thin pipe I used to wonder about. The picture on the easel was of a woman, with bare breasts plump enough to suit a figurehead. She was wearing a blue necklace. She made me feel I was sitting looking down deep into clear water, some foreign port somewhere. I was side by side with Mr Ogletree under the bow, one tin of paint hung between us as we touch up the carving. We had done with the figurehead, rouge on her cheeks and a green scarf round her long white neck; her breasts did peep out, plump and white. 'How goes it, Alf?' Nobody had the same gift for words as Mr Ogletree. He used to do letters for any seaman aboard who could not write. He would fill out their thoughts in such a way that they felt good about what they had said, although it was never word for word.

Mr Kit wore an old navy-blue denim jacket to paint in, which he had got in France. I said, if he knew French, he would like Brittany as much as Cornwall. I told him of the rocks coming into the harbour at St Mâlo, where I put in once.

I had the book Mr Ben had sent me to show him, *In the Wake of the Sailing Ships*. I said they were the same as the ones I painted.

What was it like onboard? Overall, you were better housed than you were ashore, I said. Any one of those old ships was beautiful to look at, and live on. Tell you about it? You would still be here this time tomorrow; even then you would not know it all. I had to learn by doing, and so did every other seaman. Took years before I could trot it out easy as ABC from the masthead lightning-conductors to the bilges. 'If the ship is a three-master the front is the foremast; the mainmast the middle, and the mizzenmast is astern.'

'Come aboard then, and we'll start with the fo'c'sle. Not much in the way of furniture: a scrubbed table, with benches each side. We slide it up the two wooden centre posts and peg it out of the way to make more room. Each man has his own mess locker, where he stows his goods and gear. There's a freshwater keg and a stove; we keep the coal in the forepeak store. Not much, eh? For light, we have oil-lamps on gimbals or shielded candles: green tallow mixed with rat poison.' That got a smile out of Mr Kit. 'The main freshwater tank is in the hold, and we use the pump near the mainmast; there's another pump aft in the saloon pantry.

'They always had a Board of Trade paper pinned up in the fo'c'sle that said what food a seaman could expect. Under the list was a smallprint sting in the tail that left it up to the discretion of the captain and owners. So our two ounces of butter a day could turn into margarine, or even marmalade. A quarter-pound of flour could equal four rotten potatoes, if the captain saw fit. What we hated most, though, was vinegar for lime juice. It was no cure for scurvy; nor did it make it any easier to swallow all that salt meat we ate.

'The smell when you got the lid off a cask of salt beef or pork was enough to knock you down. Each lump would weigh four pounds or so, and was bobbing in brine. The cook got it out the night before to steep it. Then he would boil it and serve it up all the colours of the rainbow – black, too – in a tin dish. It was a toss-up who got first lump, the fat with the lean.

'You ask about toilets. They were called the heads. Two on deck, one each side of the fo'c'sle. We'd flush those by hand with a can of salt water from a pump there. Those for officers were aft, built against the poop bulkheads. The captain had his own.

'What do I know about his quarters? I did my best to keep out of going there often, and I shook in my boots if I had to. He had a horsehair sofa, instrument cupboard, a bookcase, stove and mahogany table, mirrors, shelves and carvings everywhere. Everything had to be made apurpose to fit the space – even his bath. If he was musical, he might have a piano sometimes.

'How did we bathe? If the weather was fine, we used sea water in a big flat wooden tub on deck. We never left off scrubbing the decks white.

'You can never feel out of place; you are never the only short-arse aboard, see. Most crews I sailed with were small and nimble men. We washed our clothes when the weather was fine, and they would dry in no time.

'We ate in the after-deckhouse in the ship's galley. It was there that the cook, carpenter, sailmaker, bosun and petty officers had their quarters. You had a brick floor in the mess there, an iron stove with storm rails, coal and sand bins in case of fire. There was a pantry, an armoury with rifles and cutlasses, and a sail locker.

'Any man hurt went to the deckhouse for treatment; it was where the medicine chest was kept. When I think of everything I had to learn! Pins, check straps, bullock blocks, cap bands, trusses, lower-boom irons! We had a spar called hermaphrodite.'

Mr Kit laughed again, and how had that come about? What does it do? I said I did not know. It was aboard when I got there, and I had trouble enough to learn its name. Each mainmast had fife-rails with iron sockets bolted to the decking. It was the holes for the thole-pins that gave the fife-rail its name. It was one place where we would angle the spars to the wind.

'The width of a rudder would depend on the length of the ship. A rudder was good when it gave the helmsman no trouble to bring her head round.

'God forbid, but if we had to abandon ship ever, we had three boats on deck, stored on skid-beams set in chocks with lacing-pins. Back-along those days, a lifesaver came in the form of a cross with copper floats each end of the arms. The kind they have now – cork lifejackets – came later. The anchors were three kinds: Common anchors, Rodgers and Trotmans. They were kept inboard each side of the fo'c'sle. What size they were depended on the vessel's tonnage.

'If you want the sails, we can start up there with the skysail, below that comes the royal, then the single top-gallant, and under that the single topsail and lower course. Stays are the fixed ropes that go from the deck to different sections of the masts to bolster and hold them. We call the side-stays shrouds; they have ratlines, up which we go aloft to fix the sails. The yards are spars set across to the masts, on which hang the square sails. Braces are the ropes that go down from the ends of the yards to the decks. You use them to swing the yards over one side or the other, whichever way the wind is blowing. The sheets are the ropes that hold the sails' bottom corners. They take most strain when the sail is full and pulling hard.

'Sails are heavier or lighter to suit the weather. You are forever aloft to change them as the wind shifts. Go up there in the dark, in the wind, you have to know where everything is. You would know fear, Mr Kit. You would know what I mean. You are over one hundred feet up, trying not to fall off the rope you stand on while you lean across the spar to haul in sheets, white with frost. Any ropes that can tangle have, and you think you will never see the end of that sail, or get it furled. To the fore there, you would have stuns'ls royal and top-gallant and lower studding-sails. You need a good crew of men to handle all that canvas. What you could carry was up to the weather. You could spot American clippers easy; they had cotton duck-white sails. Ours were made of flax canvas, so they were grey or pale brown.'

The ship I had in mind had an iron frame with a skin of teak, oak and elm. It was painted black down to the copper sheathing that shone stem to stern as she heeled over. It had a yellow band, end to end of her hull, with brass rails fore and aft. It was a time when owners could not make up their minds to go all out for iron ships. Some owners did not give a damn for anything but speed. They wanted every inch of canvas in the worst of weather. No matter what sort of a gale was blowing, the captains they hired would padlock the sails in case the mate got cold feet and sent the crew up. They were after something for nothing, and men were drowned because of that. You rocked in your ship as in a cradle, but sometimes you were afraid it could become your grave.

One of my first jobs as a cabin boy was to ring the ship's bell on the poop every half-hour, night and day. The man on lookout at the fo'c'sle head would strike the bell there. Bells rang all the time, at the hour the watch changed over and every half-hour by two, four, six and eight bells.

To go round the Cape of Good Hope from west to east, you drop south to find the wind. If you come east to west, you have to steer well inshore so as not to run up against prevailing southerlies. You are at risk going there at all. I never want to pass that way again. Going so far south, you meet other hazards: icebergs. If there are icebergs you can bank on sleet and snow. I sit here now, with my knees up to the fire, but there, we had nothing of such comfort. The cook had the stove, and he was the only man who kept warm. The rest of us had to keep on the move or turn to ice where we stood. All I could do was try to warm my hands around a candle flame.

To flounder about there, in that awful weather, was to be in hell itself. Being small, I spent most of my time under water holding on for dear life.

Afterwards, going up the coast of Africa, you had the sweet smell of the land. You were in paradise. That perfume was everywhere aboard ship; no sea salt could scour it away.

It's never all paradise, though. You go up by Sable Island a bad time of year you may not get back. Some storms you don't live to tell about. Off Cape Hatteras the Diamond Shoals lay in wait for you to go aground on. I've voyaged that way, and found refuge in Gloucester harbour. The Virgin Mary there stands on top of the church. She is missing the baby Jesus and holds a fishing schooner instead.

A woman came in barefoot wearing a red robe. She had been swimming on Porthmeor. She began to dry her hair with a blue towel, saying how that sea had set her skin tingling and beaten away any broody hen feeling. She was sorry for what she had said. I caught only the name Frosca when Mr Kit told it.

'So, you're the Admiral,' she said.

'Alfred Wallis,' I said.

Something was not right, though, and I did not know what it was. Mr Kit was going about humming a tune, which I knew was to keep what was troubling him off his mind.

'You painted those beautiful ships we have,' she said.

Some things you have a hard time to keep up with. I felt out of my depth, and began to wish I had not come. It was too light in there; I felt I was at the bottom of a rockpool, without any shelter or shell, a queer thing.

'You won't stay for tea?'

'Best I get along now. I been here all afternoon.'

Mr Kit walked me to the corner. He said Frosca was the wife of a Polish count. She had left Russia after the revolution. She lived in a wood in the heart of Paris. 'She says I'm a creature out of a wood – a faun, perhaps; do you know about fauns, Admiral? Anyway, she is going tomorrow. I have asked my mother to come, but I think she is too ill to leave her bed.

'You start with women, you can never see an end to it,' Mr Kit said. 'You are a ship at sea, tossing between one and the other. Why is that, Mr Wallis? Frosca is one of the best, though. I depend on her. Yes, she has both feet on the ground. Were you ever married, Mr Wallis?'

'She died.'

'Only the one, then?'

If she was going back to Paris, I knew he would cry himself to sleep.

He asked, would it be too much to ask for me to write him a letter, now and then. I never did because he went off, and I never knew where he was living. Not that I would have, anyway, I'm no good at that.

'You would not think there are versions of the truth, now would you, Mr Wallis? I'm afraid there are now in this world. So many, it makes your head whirl.' He gave me a close stare. 'I envy you your sense of purpose, Admiral, your fixed belief; you are sure of your place in the scheme of things, and where you are going.'

He had something dark in him; I could not put my finger on what it was but just before I left, he spoke of two boys in Italy the terrorists had tied to the railway near

Rome. They were cut in half. Said he had seen Mussolini there, too, one day.

Mr Ben had been there with his wife, but he had gone to London. Mr Kit showed a painting where he had made them the fisherman and his family. All the seine boats were putting off from the beach, and the man was leaning near his wife and child to say goodbye.

I did not know what to say when I saw Mr Kit after Frosca had gone. How do any of us wear being alone? He was walking out on Clodgy Point with Mr Ben's wife. The blue was ebbing from the sky, and I recalled what Mr Kit had said to Frosca about the seaside being all very well, but it made a man's opium so moist he could not cook it.

Each time they pass with the dead man's chattels they darken the room. I sat a bit until they had all gone, then walked to the edge to look over Porthmeor Strand. They had the driftwood ablaze, a brisk wind beating the flames about. I felt a hand on my shoulder, and came face to face with Mr Kit. He asked what they were doing. I told him it was the custom to burn a fisherman's clothes, mattress and bedding when he died.

I did not have to read a book to know something was wrong with Mr Kit. I could feel his sadness, and felt near him, more so than any time since we met. He was there, yet he was not, if you know what I mean. We shared our devils. Nothing I could tell him about those.

When the family came up with their petrol cans, a long cloud fleeted dark along the sands. The flames blazed brighter in this, and the sea turned another colour, the waves falling white as snow.

I had nothing more to say; he smiled, and I left him there. Both of us had chosen the path we were walking.

Later that night, I went back down to the fire, which was still burning. A part of his bed, half an oar, still glowed each time the wind came. I took the oar down to the sea and threw it in. It was where it belonged. I picked up an ember to blow on and light my pipe. The dead man was Arthur Judd, the man who had warned me to fuck off home the night they beat the gypsy. As I stood smoking it came to me what I had to do. I went home and took an axe to that wardrobe with Susan on it. I was knocking it to pieces when heard her start. She was never going anyway, and I was wasting my time thinking so. I had the feeling I was disturbing her grave, but I had to keep on at it until I could carry it down to the fire. I watched her face as it began to scorch and burn; could have sworn she was smiling.

Got back home, and it was worse than ever. I had created a storm that went on all night.

Every sound a boat makes can tell you something about what will happen next, a masthead noise tells you more than any other does; eyelets in the mainsail can have an awful moan.

I said for her to go pester Jacob Ward. I said she never went over to Madron to see how he was doing, and put some flowers on his grave.

I threw a blanket over the table and got under there. It didn't stop her voice going on, but I felt safer, and fell asleep.

Mrs Peters came knocking early on. I let her come in, and she looked all around the room as if expecting to see somebody.

'You sure you're all right, Mr Wallis?'

'Why shouldn't I be?'

'Last night you did shout something awful. I thought they were murdering you.'

'They? Nobody here but me!'

She stood wiping her hands on her apron, as if she did not know what to do next. The fire was low. 'Your fire don't look too hot – you want me to boil you a kettle quick on my gas stove?'

I never saw Mr Kit again after that. I did hear that he was in Mousehole, though, two years later. He threw himself, or was thrown, under a train at Salisbury Station, Mr Ben told me.

I knew that Albert Ward had died. He must have been sixty-three, which is not a great age. They were going to put him in his wife's grave, so that she could hold him for all eternity. I had seen the funeral procession go by, then, later, they all came knocking at the door. I did not want to open it at first. They were at the window, too; so I thought I'd better get it over with.

They said they thought this of all days we could bury old hatchets, forget the bad blood.

'Bad blood is all there is left now,' I said.

They were still my children, they said.

'I got no children; they are dead.'

'You blamed Mother for them dying,' said Jessie. 'She would always say that's what you would do. We're all you got.'

I said I had caught them going through her things while she was asleep. I knew they were looking to see what she would leave them when she went. 'What do you think? That I have more money you don't know about and want to get your hands on? You've been burying a thief this afternoon.'

'If you think that, you should have got a policeman. Why is it you never did?'

'You have been the bane of my life,' I said. 'The shoal of you are alive; my seed is dead.'

'We want to help you, for Mother's sake, and for what you did for us, Alfred. There are the children. You are Granda Wallis now, no need for all these old grievances. We're all getting too old for it.'

'Who wouldn't have grievances with you bloody lot? I gave to you all, and what did Albert do to me? Did he give you all a share of what he took? I gave up half my life to seeing you were all right, and what do I have to show for it?'

Lies beget lies and suspicions. You can read it there in the Bible, page after page, in Samuel. I am washed up here, adrift without knowing where I am sometimes.

'You get that apron on, Granda Wallis and you start painting, nobody can say a word,' said Jessie. 'What did we do to you?'

'You've done nothing, you.'

'Come on, best we go now,' said Tom, never wanting it rough.

That was the end of it. I showed them the door. 'You go now. I don't feel too well. I want to get my head down.'

They went off saying I was a pedlar. I was a pedlar when they were young, going around the streets to scavenge any old thing that people wanted shot of. Sometimes they wondered if I was deaf at all, or just heard what I wanted to hear – an old cantankerous bugger, and my own worst enemy.

'I know he must be laughing up his sleeve,' said Jessie. 'He has got that London lot mazed passing off that shit he does as paintings. Gullible, I'd say.'

'Let the old sod burn in hell; it's where he wants to be,' another said.

I was glad to see the back of them.

I have never known a seaman not to suffer rheumatism in old age; now there is a ringing in my ears as well, which drives me mad. I ran some warm oil in, rolled cotton round a matchstick, but there was no wax.

You're alone, and it creeps up on you; you don't notice, then one day you find yourself reading people's lips. What I miss, though, are sounds in nature. A lark up there can sing its heart out, and I'll pass by.

I try not to hear what all the wirelesses around St Ives are saying now. I wonder those that listen to them don't get wireless brain. You hear all that whistling and moaning then music from London or Paris, or cities the other side of the world. All I think is that they are Satan's tools. He can send his messages with those. All day long those boxes tell people things, send messages. They are in the air, these messages, all around the globe, and yet they do not shed any great light. I wonder more people are not going mad. Same as eels and some other fish, we got electrics in our brain and what these wirelesses do, sending messages, is to get inside there. Or else how do we have brainwaves? What are those?

I went to see Mr Armour about the voices. Satan was at it again, I said; the Devil lived upstairs and sent his messages down the chimney. I said he had got to come round and give a hand to get shot of those.

He came with a ladder, a clock weight, a washing-line or some such, and a handful of straw. He did up the weight with straw and tied it with the line. Then he got up on the roof and let it go down the chimney. He did that three or four times, then climbed down and said, 'That's fixed it Mr Wallis, but come back and tell me if you hear any noises again.' When we went into the house, there was soot everywhere, and a heap of it beginning to smoulder in the grate. 'Call it lucky, Mr Wallis, that your chimney did not catch fire,' he said, busy with the shovel. 'You had better get a sweep in soon as you can.'

I asked him what he wanted for his trouble.

'How long have we known each other, Alfred? Say no more, say no more, you never need put your hand in your pocket for any job I do for you, especially not one easy as that.' So I gave him a painting.

I had a sheep's head and some bones boiling on the grate, so I left the door open and sat outside on a stool to cobble my shoes. It was there that I saw them coming. He said he was a friend of Mr Ede and Mr Nicholson, who had told him about my paintings. He said his name was Mr Herbert Read, and she said I must call her Barbara. She was a tall pale woman with her hair in a snood. He asked about the cobbling, and I said I had done it all my life; the work was easier now after I got a last when I was dealing.

'Jack of all trades, eh?'

'These days, I got to be one of those,' I said. 'Do yours, too, for sixpence, if you pay extra for the leather; make a proper job.'

Somebody had told them I was deaf, they spoke so loud. I had an idea they were sizing me up. He was worse than she was, with his bow-tie; a man fussing to pick every last bone out of a fish, for fear one will stick in his throat. He could afford to think he belonged anywhere in the world he happened to be standing.

When I left the sea I was a fish out of water, I said. 'I

had no place on land. I do not know myself as I was. I was nowhere until I found ships again – even then, they're paint on bits of cardboard.' Yes, that picture on the wall was of me. I was younger then. I've seen better days; I had more hair, then. I sit here so's to face the light.

'An aeroplane, an airship, alongside a sailing ship?'

'Oh yes, I seen those going over – never both together, but I should guess they might,' I said.

That three-master on the back of a calendar Miss Barbara could see. Well, the card had that shape already. 'See how nicely her spanker fits in that curve.'

'So you never trim the card?' Miss Barbara ran her finger around the shape.

'No, I never trim a card, I find my way to arranging what I want to do in there, whatever the shape is. I did a sailing ship in a rough sea with icebergs, its topsails and royals going up into cardboard the shape of a cocked hat. Just as holes in nets come in all shapes and sizes. If you can fill those, and make a proper job of it, a bit of cardboard is easy. Same as the mesh in a net, strands got to match up.'

I draw in the sails and rigging while the paint's still wet, I said.

'Isn't it because you work on a flat table that you see things the way you do?' Mr Herbert said it was about perspective.

I did not try to make him understand that wherever you are, you need a chart, and it's no different in a painting. 'No, I do it the way I do it, and I'm not changing,' I said. 'I see what I see the way I see it.'

He could put that in his pipe and smoke it.

Miss Barbara asked, 'Do you mind being on your own?'

'What I want to do is die healthy,' I said, 'but I don't see how I'm going to do that. You get sick, and people start to put your name down for the workhouse before you know it. To be old, lame and poor has been a crime since Queen Elizabeth thought up the Poor Law. When they get you into the Union, you are an outcast. All they want is for you to eat out of their hand. While I have breath in my body I will cry out the crimes of those places! All you can do is curse them, then only under your breath. Once they get you in there you lose any right. Nobody cares. Any place full to bursting, and they are, they cram you into bed head to foot with a man dying of fever. The reason there are no bodysnatchers now is that there are corpses enough in the workhouse. Of what use is all that anatomy? Medical progress, they say. Only people with money can afford doctors. Anatomy is only the cutting the butcher does to get his hands inside a pig. They use it to punish the poor, or else why draw and quarter felons for stealing a sheep? All those poor lost souls looking for their parts! Your soul hears the final trump and goes looking for your body – lo and behold, there's only half of it there!'

'I don't know whether you're serious or not, Mr Wallis,' Mr Herbert said with a laugh. 'They did away with those conditions long ago.'

'You are sure about that?'

'Things have changed for the better,' said Miss Barbara.

'A pauper will go hungry in there for fear it's his shipmates he's eating, without knowing.'

Miss Barbara does not believe such a thing.

'If a master can see his way clear to make leather out of paupers' skins, he will,' I told her. 'He has power of life and death. Charity is cold as stone. Better if Florence Nightingale had spent her time in workhouses than the Crimea. All I want, if they get me in the Union, is a quick death, because that is what people in there pray for. It is the last stop on the way to the grave.'

Mr Herbert did not have much time for that. 'The only sea I know anything about is the North Sea,' he said. He had heard that if he could sail close enough, he would see the barbed wire left over from the war on the Flanders coast. I said I never liked to sail there. I had been there in bad weather once; it kept with us all the way south, past Flamborough Head. Then a gusty blow forced us into the Humber. There the waves came even faster. A stiff westerly began to blow, stiff enough to make us think what to do with night coming on. We had the tiller lashed tight over, for the tides are always bad there. We put the hook down off Paull, sheeted the jib for weather, and ran up a riding-light. We could just about see the Bull lightbuoy and the light at Spurn. The storm blew all night; then at dawn, in the grey, I could hear the sad ting-tang of the rods striking the bell. I never did pass a bell at sea but it sounded mournful.

I made out a barge on the sandbank. 'No, she's not stranded,' said Clem. I could see four men then, digging in the sand, either side the keel, shovelling it for dear life into the hold. The skipper smoked his pipe under a big umbrella and watched them sweat. 'Sandies, they call them,' said Clem. 'Between tides they'll get out thirty to forty tons. Those men are throwing that sodden sand six feet up into that hold. If the barge is any higher, they run half-way up a hatch to get it aboard. The deeper the spit both sides of the keel, the higher they must throw. I'd say that was bloody hard labour. They sell the load for ballast to ocean-going ships in Hull.'

I cared even less for that coast below Harwich; there were shoals everywhere. The Lemon and Ower sands north-east of Cromer, the Wash itself – then a maze of backwaters, rivers, creeks and saltings. 'It is all barges there, big ungainly things laden down with all kinds of stuff: coal, worzels, wheat, bricks and hay. You give those a wide berth; some of the skippers are mad old buggers.'

Mr Herbert began to say that every person they had spoken to about me said, when I cut across his bow.

'Why did you talk about me? You got no need talking to other people about me. All they're going to tell you are lies. You want to know anything you come to me. I'm the only one who knows. Those others persecute me, and are jealous, put it about now that I was never at sea at all, and that's a lie. That's the worst thing anybody could find to say behind my back. I paint every ship I ever saw afloat.'

He had his back turned when I told Miss Barbara to mind what company she kept.

She laughed, and said he was a famous art critic who could help to get my name known in the art world. He was staying with her where she lived, in Carbis Bay.

'I don't often go that way – do crab apples still grow along the way to Hayle?'

She picked up the cloth with purple spots I use to cover over the melodion; said she had never heard one of those. I got it onto my knee and began to play 'Lead, Kindly Light'. Mr Herbert let his head go back and forth as if he knew the tune and could sing the words, but I don't think so. I made a joke about my wife, saying, 'You can't get up to the Salvation Army to sing. Don't sing here.' I could laugh now about that.

'The black book is Mildred Duff's *Life of Christ*,' I said, 'it belonged to my wife. I keep the Bible under there, close by, in a box. It is the Bible that has been in my family for years, my chart to Heaven. Not a day goes by but what I read some of it. You open the Bible to read to pass the time. Some texts you know by heart, yet I have to say the words, to utter them forth. It's not a newspaper, where you read about men dying and it don't mean anything, and there is a picture of the bridegroom in the other woman's bed.'

Miss Barbara tried to hide a smile, but I saw it.

'We have taken up too much of your time, Mr Wallis,' Mr Herbert said, shaking my hand. 'Thank you for putting up with the questions we've pestered you with.'

I sold Miss Barbara a picture of the Old House and Porthmeor Square. I said it was St Ives in the dark days. That's the square there you can see from my house.

Mr Herbert had a leather purse in his pocket, and went over to the window to count out the right amount.

I turned away, wanting them out of it now, and he sensed that and came closer. I was not happy after that until I got them on the doorstep and all was calm again. Outside, Mr Herbert stared across at Clodgy and said St Ives was such a lovely place to live in. Anybody who looked at that view, the bay, the Island, and Godrevy winking there would say the same. 'I have met with few artists with a surer sense of where they live,' he said. 'You hold it all in the palm of your hand.'

'Easy enough to picture that,' I said.

He said there were few satisfactions greater than being an artist.

'No, I don't see that I'm an artist,' I said. 'I try to make everything go in harmony, if that's the word. Some days, though, I feel too calm to paint, calm in the wrong way.'

I said I knew about artists, though; I had seen them often in Newlyn. 'Soon as a net-loft fell empty, there was an artist in it,' I said. 'When work was slack, there was one would get fishermen out on the sands, dressed in Drake's doublets and hose to point the way to the New World.'

Mr Ben had come to St Ives and called in to see how I was doing. He would write where he was living in Dulwich, and I sent him paintings there. Now he was trying to tell me something I did not want to hear – something everybody had to understand. There had been an awful disaster that struck all over the world. 'Banks are closing their doors, men jumping to their death out of windows,' he said, 'all because of a crash on Wall Street.'

Was that the night Susan came with three of her dead cronies? They were praying in the corner there, or so I thought at first, until they turned their heads to look at me. They were laughing and smiling, sharing some joke that I was a short-arse. 'Go on, go on, why don't you? Bring in the whole band of dead Salvationists and have done with it,' I shouted.

Sweat stood out on my brow; I felt I had been beaten with rods. I did not know why I was being punished. What had I done? I stuck by her, as a man does. I lay back in the box. My eyes were open, I could see, but I could not lift my hand or move a muscle. Strangest of all, my eyes were abrim with tears that would not stop coming. How long I lay that way I had no idea. When I could get up, the pillow was soaked. My head felt hot, and began to ache; I tied a damp towel round it.

Daylight was coming on. Next thing I see was a shadow on the lace curtain where I lie on the couch. It's Jacob. He delivers the letters; that's his job. He used to whistle along and knock, hoping to get in for a mug of tea. He doesn't bother to try it now, with things as they are, but I see him think what a letter is about before he puts it through the door. I see him looking at a letter he brought from Mr Ede. As I wrote to Mr Ede, when I sent him some pictures: 'The most you get is what used to be – all I do is out of my memory. I do not go out anywhere to draw. I never see anything I send you now, it is what I have seen before.'

If Mr Ede or Mr Ben do not write, I write to them. I'm not a toy rattle to pick up and put down whenever it suits them. What I hate most is when they send paintings back. How do I know why they think one is better than another is? I don't see any difference.

It's easier if I get Mr Armour to read Mr Ede's letters.

'Mr Ede says he'd like to visit St Ives one day, but his job at the gallery keeps him busy. He hopes to see you sometime, meanwhile you must look after your health. He encloses a cheque for three pounds so that you can have a good Christmas.'

The *Cecilia* was unloading coal at the pier. The weather turned rough, and I saw her break loose and smash her way out of the harbour. She hit almost every vessel lying there as she carried out into the bay and onto the rocks of Pedn Olva. She was a ketch, and the last sailing ship I saw come to grief.

Not long after that, Mr Adrian and his wife came to live in Carbis Bay, at Parc Owles. Mrs Margaret was born in Wu-Kung, China. They have all come a long way it seems to fetch up here. The flowers she had brought were for me, she said.

What was I to do with those? If I had no vase, where was there a pail she could put them in?

She was doing that when she asked me if I ever went to the Scala to see a film.

'A picture-house? No, I never been in one of those, and I don't want to.'

'You never know, you might get to like it. I go; I find it better than staring at my four walls in the winter.'

'I got more than a fair share of shadows,' I said.

She took my hand suddenly before I could pull back and looked at my palm. 'What would you like to be if you could live your life over again? Would you be painting earlier?'

'If I had not been born where I was, and the man I am, I might have had a different life, I think. I cannot guess how it could have been, though. No. I'd go to sea again, if I could get a berth aboard a sailing ship.'

Thinking of this gave me enough of a glow to ask if she would drink a cup of tea.

'Can't I make it?'

'Not in my house. I do things here.' I got the tea caddy down. 'You sit still.'

'Tell me about Mrs Wallis. She is very stern in that photograph, if it's of her, is it?'

'Don't want to talk about her,' I said.

It would have meant it all coming up again. The thought of losing that money never goes away, it's always at the back of my mind. That's when Albert took it, a bit at a time, when he brought clean sheets back. Then, lo and behold, one day there was none left to take.

Mrs Margaret would not want to hear about that.

They wanted my work, and I was glad of that, but they could have landed from the moon for all I knew about them, with their wives and children.

'Let me take your picture,' she said, going out into the road. 'Come out into the light, or I can't do it properly.'

So I came out as far as the door and stood there in the sunlight.

All I had left of family was my nephew Billy, Charlie's son. They came then one day around Christmas time and said wouldn't it be better if I went to live with them. I would find more to do and have more people to talk to. Well, I did; I packed up and went over there. No, it did not suit me at all. A woman will always run a house in her own fashion, and Billy's missus was the same. If I wanted food, it was on the table at meal times. And, if I weren't there, I would have none at all. I don't blame her, but I was too set in my ways to let hunger tie me down to a timetable.

I got out of Billy's house so fast I never said goodbye. I cleared my gear out and set off to walk. I was at Marazion having a bit of a rest when I heard the car horn. It was Mr Adrian going home to Carbis Bay. He asked did I want a ride to Back Road.

Driving along, I asked him if he knew Colonel Benson and his daughter. I told him where the bungalow was. He said no, so far as he knew, the people living there now had nothing to do with India. The man had a wife, but no daughter, and was more likely to be a retired accountant than anything military.

I asked if he would like to come in and see the new painting I had done.

'Consols Mine, Rosewall Hill and the road you can see is to Zennor and those farms around there,' I said. 'The white is granite showing. It was the Germans had put a lot of money into it, so mining there fell off when the war started.

'I would not work down a mine for all the tea in China,' I said. 'What you hear first is the thump of the great beam-engine. It hisses up and down as it lifts gallons of water from the shaft that runs out undersea. You think it would be cold, but it can be hot as hell going down all those ladders. Everywhere the rock is leaking water, and dank as the grave; you feel you are in the chimney of a ruined cottage. At the bottom, if you have the courage to reach it, you can hear the hollow moan and crash of the sea as it breaks a hundred feet and more above. Up-along there is where the miners lived.'

'You sound as if you knew them,' said Mr Adrian. 'I thought they kept themselves apart up there.'

'He was called John Furze,' I said. 'As a boy, he had to wheel a full barrow from the workings along on a plank in the dark. Often he couldn't hold it from tilting so that he tore the skin off his hands on the walls. "See the scars, here," he would say, holding them out. What you got down there, if something else didn't kill you, was hookworm. Those buggers got under your skin and burrowed their way into your guts, where they would suck out your blood.'

Tin, lead, copper, silver, iron nitrates, I don't know what they did not dig out of the earth around here. It was the tin from Bolivia and Malaya that could be got easy that knocked all that on the head.

The price of black tin fell. They were getting it easier in Malaya and Bolivia than lode-mining here. St Ives Consols shut down, but they had it going again in 1908. I saw Rosewall at work then. Nothing runs smooth. The Consols mine was bankrupt; the miners had to go off and fight the Kaiser's men. William Harvey of Hayle got all the ore from Bolivia. Mind you, with the German blockade he got little or none, so he took a share in an American smelter.

I'd say I weigh nine stone, near enough, but beside Mr Furze I was a giant. After he was down the mine, he had lived a sorry life. He had gone to work for Harvey's in Hayle, there, where he had breathed so much arsenic, ladling liquid metal from furnace to mould, that he was a walking skeleton. His two small children tended him hand and foot to stay alive. They knew they were orphans for the workhouse when he died. The foundry was killing him slowly, only he had not known it. 'They do it quicker now on relief,' he said.

It was January, and George V died the same day. At first, I thought the letter was from Mr Ede, but I knew it wasn't soon as I had a whiff of the perfume. It was from the woman who came to see Reuben. She had not killed him, she said, but felt she had. When she left he was alive, but in a poor way. She had not wanted to go, but he had forced her. She had never liked hurting him, but he had paid her to do it. She had to number each lash, speak it aloud. She did not want to say how many. She was sorry he had died. He had often talked about his friend Mr Wallis, and had shown her my cottage one time. The years had gone by. She was near the end now, and did not want to die with that business on her mind. She was too ashamed to admit it to a priest, and I was the only person she felt she could tell.

Who could I talk to about the letter? Mr Hollow was dead, and I did not know how to tell Mr Armour. He had known Reuben Sadd, and would not believe he could have done those things. So I let it go. There was nothing I could do for the woman, even if I could find her.

Going up where the sky waits at the top of the Digey, I did

not hear the Mayor's car coming until I was thrown under it. You used to have to look alive not to get crushed under a wagonload of casks along Fore Street. If there was one horse-and-cart coming down there, there were five I had to watch out for. At least you could hear those. As I lay there, I had a flash of General Booth's saintly face, not knowing where or who I was. Neither the Mayor nor his wife got out to see whether I had any broken bones. You would think I was some stray dog they had run down. I was eighty-two. My mouth tasted as if I had sucked some rusty iron from those fumes in my face. They didn't bother to say, are you hurt, do you want us to take you to the doctor? The driver had some smelling salts from the woman he held under my nose. He helped me up and brushed me down. Both of them were looking through me, as if I had been holding out my cap to beg a shilling.

I keep out the road now. I wrote about it all to Mr Baughan, and he said it was a disgrace. I told him how it crept up behind me. My insides were shaken in and out, and I cannot stand any knocking about. I won't forget how testy the Mayor was: 'He's all right now, get back behind the wheel. Come along!' I wrote and told Mr Ede about it, too.

That night Susan came out of the shadow into the light of the oil-lamp. She was wearing her Army hat, and had her hymnbook in her hand. I was waiting for her to sing, but that was not why she had come. She told me that the world was going to end in three days' time, and I had to get down on my knees and prepare my soul. 'All you came ashore with was a handful of dreams,' she said. 'If I had not put my foot down, you would never have left the sea. The time is over for lazing about abeautifying bits of

cardboard all day – ships going out, ships coming home to
harbour . . .'

'Stop talking to me,' I said, 'I don't want to hear any
more!'

'Wool-gatherer!' she said.

'You can't wool-gather when you're roped to a yard-
arm in a gale!' I shouted.

Ever after that she was Duty Mighty, and kept on at me
at night. Who could I turn to, where could I find anyone
to gainsay that power?

I went to Mr Armour; somebody was sure to have told
him, anyway. I expect the whole town knew how touched I
am. Seeing him stood by his cashbox made it all seem just
a bad dream, but I had to tell him. I said I'm not going to
do any more painting.

'No painting at all? Why is that, Mr Wallis?'

'Duty Mighty has set it down in the tables of the law.'

'Who might Duty Mighty be?'

'It's a voice I hear of a night. Says I'll get hell if I paint.' I
was not going to tell him it was Susan coming to get at me.

'Sounds as if Duty Mighty is a woman. Am I right?'

Mr Armour was always sharp.

'Pay no mind to what she says, Mr Wallis,' he said.
'Obey me: you must paint all you want. Never mind her at
all.'

'One is never enough,' I said. 'What I mean is, I have to
do another, and then more. Is that a sin? Like those
Israelites kneeling to that gold calf? I like to touch the
paint sometimes, to get it perfect, and feel so good about
it. Maybe Duty Mighty is right; maybe I ought to deny
myself that pleasure?'

'You got to try to put Susan out of your mind, Mr
Wallis; for I know it's her you're talking about. Defy that

Duty Mighty! A chapter has closed, and you have to let her rest in peace.'

'That's easier said than done.'

Before I left, he read me the letter Mr Ede had sent to ask me whether I felt any better after being knocked down. He said he had given a lecture about my pictures in America, and nobody would speak to him after that. But never mind; time was going to tell, and my paintings would be under glass in galleries for years to come.

My father came to see me last night. He had on the uniform he wore in the Crimea and it stank of gunpowder. His tunic was muddy; so were his boots. He propped his musket against the mantelpiece and turned the chair round to sit facing me, filling his pipe with my tobacco. When you start to see your dead father, where does that leave you?

I heard Father say, 'He was already running faster than we saw him ever run before, and we all cheered and swore that he would reach the trench. Then he tripped and fell, had time for one last, sad look at us before the cannon-ball sent him to kingdom come. It left only bits and pieces that none of us had the heart to go out and find when the guns were silent.' He made no sign of moving, puffing his pipe, until suddenly there was another soldier there, leaning on the mantelpiece to stare into the coals. He was looking at cards he held in his hand. 'I got such good makings here, Charlie, we can't lose. It's getting late, though. Time we moved along. We should be some other place.'

I lend Mr Baughan the book Mr Ben gave me: 'To Alfred Wallis from Ben Nicholson'. I thought he had a right to share in that a bit. On a Friday, when I was in his shop to buy groceries, I would lay it on his counter and leave it. Nothing said until he would ask when I wanted it again.

Then I went out to Clodgy, where I saw the sign: an arrow made up of pebbles on the path. You come across messages in the strangest of places. The wind was lashing wisps off the sea, but not strong enough to set a real swell running. Just chipping away. It was blowing the sand up, too. When I came back, I walked across the beach where the tide had left dry dogfish egg cases strewn about. Soon as I got up to the road, I looked and saw a gang of Boy Scouts coming along. I kept going as far as I dared, but they had staves and were looking for trouble. I could see it in their faces. They had such hairy legs they could end in cloven hoofs. The noise they made coming was worse than a press-gang. I knew they were Baden-Powell's imps of Satan sent by Duty Mighty to get me. That woman is fell, and she will do anything to threaten my life. I got back inside the house, slammed the door and locked it quick. I was right to do that; two of them soon came at the window trying to look in. I don't care what Mrs Peters say about they had some jamboree on the Island. Why they come after me, then, looking in my house to see where I was hiding?

I had banked the fire up, but it had gone out. I crumpled paper, laid sticks and cinders, coaxing and blowing until I got a flame, then I held a paper across the chimneybreast. I could hear the wind roar in the flue. Soon as the paper glowed orange and began to char, I took it down and thrust the poker into the cinders to open them up a bit. When I had a proper flame, I looked at the boat I had painted on the bellows that hung on the wall there.

In the dark, I see her come along the deck in her

wedding gown and throw white flowers in the sea. The skipper ran after her like he was sixteen again and not a forty-year-old. The first thing she did was to wash all his clothes, and they were dry before we were out of sight of land. The skipper had his jacket off the next few days, walking around the deck in his shirtsleeves, showing his shirt off, I reckon. Mind you, I never saw her wash anything again after that. Of course, none of the crew had wanted her aboard at first. Then they all tried to find something to do astern when she sat there in her deckchair, just to get a sniff of her perfume. They liked to hear her play the piano, and she knew that and would leave the hatch open. She brought a sewing-machine aboard with her, and the dresses she made were as good as those in a shop window. I remember one red dress she wore, and I thought of her soon as I saw one like it floating after a wreck. There was everything afloat: chests and boxes, and that red dress. Lots of stuff came ashore after the *Alba* sank, too, old newspapers, clothes and bottles and such.

I was on the beach to see her driven ashore on the rocks of the Island with the loss of six lives. She was out from Barry with a cargo of coal bound for Italy. I painted her maybe a dozen times, with the lifeboat *Caroline Parsons* thrown up on the rocks beside her. She was the first boat to have an engine. All her crew survived.

There was an oil-slick washing coal dust up the beach for weeks.

No longer in that line, I could see a way to make some money from her, rusting out there. The sea set her clanging again at high water. There was salvage coming ashore; I went down to the edge of the sea, but there were too many people about, two policemen, a parson I had never seen before had his prayerbook open. He had a nurse to hold his hat. She had tied on a yellow sou'wester. No matter how long I waited, or how many times I went back, there was always somebody there.

Padstow sent a boat to replace the *Caroline Parsons*. I was trying to sleep while a north-west wind blew. It was the worst since 1890. The wind was howling in the chimney. At two o'clock in the morning, an S.O.S. came in from Cape Cornwall. The gusts there were over ninety miles an hour. A steel-screw steamer, the *Wilston*, heading for La Goulette with coal, was in trouble. The Sennen lifeboat was nearest, but they could not launch her because the tide was low. It took eighty men in St Ives to wrestle our boat out of the harbour. That was the *John and Sara Eliza Stych*. They never saw her again except the flare she fired at twenty past four. She had capsized, and half her men went over the side – coxswain, bowman, signal-man and a crewman. The four men left were swept towards Godrevy. The engine stalled after a rope fouled the propeller, and there came more big waves that hit her beam, and she went over again taking the motor man and the other two. The third time she rolled over, the last man, William Freeman, was thrown onto the Strap Rocks at Gwithian. It was his first time out in a lifeboat. He saw the *John and Sarah Eliza Stych* strike the rocks, then got ashore and stumbled off to a farmhouse.

By then the *Wilston* lay on the Longships reef, her back broken, with thirty men lost. Every flag in St Ives flew at half-mast; the houses were hung with black, the bell tolling. Nobody can do a thing about those times. I heard William Freeman tell his story. The coxswain's missus lost both her husband and son. One widow was pregnant, and eight children lost a father. Mr Freeman got the Institution's bronze medal, and so did the six dead men. They tell me the wireless people came to get his story. When people heard it here, they said it was very moving.

The best I could do was save three weeks' pension money for the Lifeboat Fund towards the boat they got next.

We stood to watch the smoke as they burned the *John and Sarah Eliza Stych* under Godrevy Head. Seeing Mr Hesp come down the beach, I turned to him and said, 'Those Padstow lifeboats got no luck at all. A day as grey as this in 1900 they went out in the *James Stevens*. It was the first steam lifeboat, and it had a hell of job even to clear the harbour. Every man was putting his life at risk to help the *Peace and Plenty*, a Lowestoft trawler that had drifted onto Doom Bar. God alone knows how the other lifeboat *Arab* had got to where the trawler was foundering. Three of the trawlermen were dead; five others hurt when a lifesaver rocket fell among them. The *Arab* went under a wave that took her eight men and oars over the side. They got back in place with three oars left. Her coxswain must have had God's hand on his to guide the gig into an inlet. The rocks there broke every oar like a matchstick except one, tore a hole in her side, and made tinder of her rudder.'

If I feel low I go down by the sea and stand awhile to listen to it come and go until I'm still. But then, up to my ankles was not enough. The wind was beating spray off the waves and I felt I had to get out there in it, to let it lift me up and let me fall. I cut the legs off my old trousers, got my clothes off and set out. It was cold, but I soon got used to it, although I had trouble keeping my footing among those rollers. I swam out a bit and turned on my back to see Barnoon. I began to think it might be a good way to go, swim out as far as I can, then let the sea do the job – why not? I had been cheating it all these years. I felt drawn to that notion, even let myself sink under a bit, just to see, but I gave myself a fright.

So I came round to face the beach and saw the children throwing my raincoat about. I took in water shouting at them and began to fight my way ashore. Kezia had put the coat on and was running up and down, with the lads egging her on. All I could see were those shadows of herself she left behind. The faster she ran, the more there were. I was out of the water by then, shivering as I spread my arms wide to catch her. She came on laughing, then took a step to the side to pelt through the sea suds and flung my coat in my face. The wind blew it over my head, a button stung my cheek and I fell on my knees in the surf. When I got my head free, all I could see were her footprints fading in the sand.

I thought she had gone, then I saw Alice Fincher, clear as day, only she was never there at all, only Kezia who said, 'Give us a squeeze, why don't you, you dirty old man? I see that look in your eye. I'm no Duty Mighty!'

'Who told you about her? Who told you that?'

Kezia walked away, looking back over her shoulder as if to make sure I would follow.

It came flying out of the dark. At first, I thought it was a gull about to strike, but as I fought it off my face, I knew it was a newspaper. In black letters, it said 'Munich Talks'.

I read in the *West Briton* that the police are breaking miners' heads in Pool. The mining company will not have the Transport and General Workers' Union asking forty-five

shillings a week for its members. The union men are
on strike while the company pays the blacklegs extra to
work South Crofty. The union blacks all tin out of the
mine. None of the dockers at any port will handle it. The
company is trying to get it out on the sly at Gweek, a dead
port hidden away on the Helford River. Twenty-eight
lorries take the tin there to a Dutch coaster. The union
men are ready to fight. The men break the windscreens of
the lorries, and the police set about hitting them again.

When I hunted round to see what I could pawn, I went
into the chest and saw those few double sheets that Albert
had left, and I had never used after Susan died – not that
they would fetch much. I rigged up a line to air them one
by one in the passage. The morning I made up a parcel
there had been rain, and there were signs that there was
more coming. Not wanting the sheets wet, I got on the
train to Penzance.

This railway was not long built when I came here. I used
to see throngs of the drunken navvies who made it go
along the pubs in Penzance. In those days, you could look
down and the harbour was full of sails: schooners, gigs and
luggers.

Mostly I walk if I go to Penzance, but I don't mind a
train-ride sometimes, if I got business. Not that day,
though.

The last time I ran up against them was on Skidden
Hill, and the time before that at a meeting. The next time I
see them, they were kicking a ball around on the Island
and began name-calling and using bad language. Then
they were ganging up there near Tregenna, with the trees
hung heavy and golden in late summer. I had picked up a
bitter acorn to chew, fit only for pigs, they tell me. It was
late on in the year; the berries were bloat with tasteless

juices, a nest of insects. I was happy till those lads came charging about.

Now they kept craning up in front of me to use the mirror on the wall above the seat where I was sitting. How could they be the same lads I had seen on Porthgwidden those years ago? I did not know how that could be so. I pushed them away and told them to sit on the seats.

'You old arsehole,' said one.

I can't say why, but children have been calling me names ever since I lived at Bethesda Hill, going round the streets.

'You got a lot of ill will between you!' I said. 'Why? What did I ever do to any of you?'

He said my old woman gave him hell at Sunday school.

When the train stopped at Lelant, I tried to get out, but two of them, taunting, got between the door and me. Then I heard doors slam and the guard blew his whistle. I took a look at the communication cord, and the penalty for improper use. It was a fine I couldn't afford, so I had to sit still, and pay no mind to their antics.

Damn and blast it! Coming home it was the same thing. They had seen me get in and waited till the very last minute the guard blew his whistle. Then they came jumping in to where I was sitting, falling over and laughing their heads off. Well, I wasn't going to have it again all the way to St Ives. When the train stopped at Marazion I got out, shouting, 'You bloody imps of Satan!'

The guard stared at me as I went past. I told him I was buggered if I was going to ride on his train if he let those pests on.

Mrs Peters came in to tell me that Jessie was dead. 'They

are burying her in three days' time. Will you go, do you think?'

'They send you along here to find that out?'

'Not at all; not at all, Mr Wallis,' she said. 'I got some idea how things are between you, and so does everybody else here. A family's quarrels are none of my concern. I leave well alone. You can't win there. I know you got poisoning on your mind all the time. No Ward, so far as I see, would ever want to harm you, but if you got it in your head, you will come down hard on anybody.'

I went up Barnoon before the Salvation Army brought her body there. I stood looking down into the hole, and I could see her as the child she was when I first met her, and it all came back. I stood a ways off when they all came. 'All you need do is ask,' she had said. 'A few things of yours to wash won't make any upset to my load. Just bundle them up and I'll take them along. I'll iron them fresh, too.'

She was always the one to speak her mind, short and sharp, whether you would agree with her or not. I never thought she would ask for a share in the money Albert stole, not her; but I was so angry with them I could not treat one any different, or they would all creep back. Married to Mr Williams' son, Tom, I did not believe he would have let her take a penny of that money.

Never mind that, from now on I keep a good watch. A lookout has to go from one side of the ship to the other for two hours, to keep an eye on the lights, red to port, green to starboard. What he looks for is anything out of the way, a light, or a sound of any kind, at any of which he will call out to the officer of the watch. Four men work while the rest sleep on deck if the weather is fair, at the ready for anything. There were some things you saw you did not talk about, for fear your shipmates put you down as mad.

'Sometimes you see them so clear they seem real,' I told Mr Baughan. 'The fo'c'sle watch calls out a ship is passing, then you hear the midshipman cry out on the quarterdeck, but she will vanish before she comes along your side.'

I boiled up pans of water and got in the bath in front of the fire and sang

> *Our boots and clothes are all in pawn*
> *It's flaming draughty round Cape Horn,*
> *Go down you blood red roses go down*
> *O you pinks and posies Go down you blood red roses go down*
> *O you pinks and posies Go down you blood red roses, go down.*

The first thing you learn on a sailing ship is to haul in time with the others. I was hauling with a will with the best of them, the wind in my ears. I knew to pull on the right word and keep good time, if we were to get where we were going. All that steam was still wreathing around as I got out, so I could not be sure what I was seeing. It came to me that Duty Mighty had hold of Kezia's hand. The girl was older now, and naked. I could see her little breasts and a tuft of hair below. She was wetter than a seal; water ran off her breasts so they had an unholy glitter of wet peaches. I knew at once what Duty Mighty was after. She had all the temptations of that girl's flesh on show. What did she think she would get me to do to the child?

All at once, the light in the room did change; I felt I was drowning, I was choking. I was breathing sea water, and my lungs were full of it. It happens when you hang a man; his cock jerks up stiffer than a steel bolt, and so did mine. My cry was bubbles, while my blue jellyfish sperm floated in strings across the sunken cabin and Kezia swam about with a grin. Behind her, in the shadows, Susan went to and fro, sometimes a seal, other times a shark.

I opened the door a crack when I heard the knocking. There was a policeman in a wet cape, shining his lantern in my face. 'Who is that with you, Mr Wallis? Is there somebody in there hurting you?' He made to get by and come inside, but I stood my ground, the sweat cold on my body.

'Nobody here except me,' I said, looking round behind. The room was usual, no Kezia floating in the air naked, and no Duty Mighty to see anywhere.

'You are up late,' he said. 'It's two in the morning. I was passing on my beat when your neighbours said they had heard you shouting and moaning. I looked in and saw you by the fire.'

'What was I doing?'

'Only talking to yourself and smoking your pipe. The room was full of smoke.'

I looked out across the road and made out Sarah Rainford and another woman in their nightdresses.

'That's not against the law,' I said.

Mr Edwards had a poem to show me. A poet who lived in St Ives had left him it. It was about a watch.

> *I lift you up from the mantel*
> *Piece here in my house*
> *Wearing your verdigris.*
> *At least I keep you wound*
> *And put my ear to you*
> *To hear Botallack tick.*

Then he asked what did I think about us having to go to war again.

'With Germany?'

'Yes, Germany.'

'They didn't finish the last one; that's how I know. All right then, what month, what day, is it?'

'You don't know?'

'I don't care, anyway.'

I did not have any time to listen to that. I had too much on my mind. I can never get rid of those voices. There is nothing Mr Armour or anybody else can do to shut them up. You would think she had done enough of that while she was alive. She was forever on at me about one thing or another. I did stand by her; I did my duty – no man, not Jacob Ward, did it better.

I was outside the shop talking with Mr Armour when Mr White came along with a cartload of springs out of beds and chairs. I had to look away, go back inside the doorway a bit. 'What's amiss, Mr Wallis?'

'Don't you know White is one of them?' I said. 'You may think those are bed springs he has in his cart, but no matter what shape they are they're wires they use in a wireless. Look how he treats that horse; it's as thin as a rake. I better get indoors to Mr Edwards until he's gone.'

I ran the tap and washed my face in the pail. It was a fair day. Lacing up my boots, I thought I might step along to Penzance. I went to look at Mr Swail's lodgings, where he had died long ago. I went up to Morrab Gardens and sat awhile on the bench where we used to spin our yarns. Coming out of there, I went on down past Humphrey Davy where he stood keeping a weather eye on all the sinners toiling up Market Jew Street, where Wesley used to preach.

Clouds rose up as I took a turn on the Esplanade.

Outside the cinema was a poster on a stand, a woman leaning up to a man with a house on fire behind; *Gone With the Wind* it said. All my life I have lived with the wind. I have gone with it to far places, and it has blown me home again. I have fought to go against it when it was doing its best to kill me. You have to learn to ride every adverse wind, tacking, easing your way along. You drift willy-nilly when the winds are contrary, nor all your rage nor prayer can make a jot of difference or turn them to the quarter you desire. There are winds that blow so hard you can't breathe, unless you turn your head away. Others come steady enough; those are the trades. Unless you were being pushed along on a trade wind, you could expect trouble of one sort or another. It was never plain sailing. I'm thinking now of those nasty squalls that stammer as they hit the sails smack, smack, and so hard you feel each blast will rip a hole in them.

A girl came up with a man and she hauled him over to see the poster, which she knew all about. She told him what millions it had cost to make the film, and who was in it. That was Clark Gable, and they had just found the actress who was playing Scarlett O'Hara. It would be years before they showed it in Penzance, and she longed for it to come. She wished that they could go in and see it now, for it was the picture of a lifetime. I did not like the way she turned sadly to stare across the bay at Michael's Mount. She was like that girl who knelt behind me in the Salvation Army photograph. I forget her name, if I ever knew it. To look at her you would think she was abstemious, but she could move her lips like a bird, to made a sucking sound, as if she was pleading for a kiss.

I went across to pass water. Soon as I got my fly buttons open in the urinal – there it was. I could see blood trickling down the stall; I was pissing blood. I stood there, I could not bear to look at it, but you pass blood out of your body, you can look nowhere else except up to the heavens. It was suddenly dark up there, too, and a great cloudburst came that drove the rain in on me.

I ran holding a newspaper over my head, a washed-out rat. I got under a shop blind alongside two old tearful women. The shopkeeper came out and got them inside. I dare say he was hoping to sell them something. The sea had changed colour in a squall; the waves came bursting up over the front.

Is this any sort of a life for a man to be living, I had to ask myself, walking the melancholy road home. The blood ran three days. Just when I got my courage up to see the doctor, it went away.

Mrs Israels came today. She called herself Miriam. She said she was married to a Russian sculptor. She had real glasses under her sunglasses and wore a yellow straw hat. I did not like it that I couldn't see her eyes. She said Mr Adrian had told her about my paintings and she was keen to buy some for the bungalow they had rented in Carbis Bay. She was pregnant. She wanted a daughter, she said, and she would call her Nina-Serafina.

I was too tired to talk much, and her handwriting was hard to make out. They had been set on going to America, but there were no berths to be had aboard a ship.

She looked at all my pictures a long time, asking how I made up such beautiful colours.

'Why, it's yacht paint I use; it's for the boats, see,' I said, surprised she couldn't see that. 'Colour is different things. Fish use colour to hide; I use it to remember days that have passed away – men and their ships and places that are gone. This one here is the seine house, with the seine boats abreast on the sand behind the pier. I felt sad that day about it, so maybe that's why I did it blue and grey, the boats black as dead bean pods. What the colours are depend on how I feel or what I have to hand. The sea is all kinds of colours. It can be red; you can sail all day, and by night it still glows red. Sometimes, nights just before winter, it can burn bright as day; you got a wake the colour of milk. Yet you hold up a jar of sea water, and it has no colour at all.'

The picture she was looking at was the Hold House in the Square across there, I said. 'You can see over to the Island behind it. I done St Ives Bay and Godrevy more times than I can remember. I did one with a schooner with yellow sails, I recall.'

I get eight shillings for a big one, and go down in price if they are small. Mr Ede used to send five pounds when he bought a bundle. 'I've made the cheque out for five pounds, to tide you over,' he would write. Mr Baughan or Mr Armour used to cash his cheques. Right ho, Mr Ede, I would say to myself, let's not sink the ship for a ha'p'orth of tar. That was before he went to live in Morocco.

'They exploit you,' said Mrs Israels. 'You deserve more than a few shillings for three or four paintings. Paintings they talk about in the same breath as Picasso. I don't care who they are. Why do art-lovers like to see artists as paupers? Do they think of destitution as a spur?'

'Don't know any Picasso,' I said.

'He is a painter, and he is not poor, Mr Wallis. He has money. I have no idea what your work is worth, or what will become of you. They think well of themselves all the same; they can all afford more than they pay you!'

'I gave them away to people, and I suppose they threw

them out. I did some on marmalade jars; the paint goes nicely on glazes. I got plenty of others. What they do, they come in and see a painting they like, hand over what they think, and I wrap it in newspaper. So I don't know what to say. Mr Ede used to say – '

'What Mr Ede said or didn't say is not something I want to discuss,' she said, sharpish.

'Do you know Mr Ede?' I asked.

'I don't have to know him,' she said.

To calm her down, I said that she was one of the few people I knew in St Ives I could talk to. 'The pity of it is that we can talk only with the living, and only then when we speak a language both of us can understand,' I said. 'You ought to know, you are a worse foreigner than I am.'

At that, we both had a laugh.

'That's where I fail,' I said, 'so nowadays I talk mostly to my mother, or myself.'

She gave me four shillings, saying she and Mr Naum didn't have a lot of money between them, but they were luckier than those Jews left in Europe. She said Mr Ben and Miss Barbara had been at her wedding.

I kept one shilling and gave the others back. Told her, her needs were greater than mine were, she had a baby coming.

If she was not going to have the responsibility of a child, Mrs Israels said she would take care of me. I shook my head hearing this.

Someone was knocking on the door; it was my nephew, Billy, come round to find out what the matter was. 'Why did you leave us not knowing where you'd gone?'

'Well, you found me again, Billy.'

'So I did, and I don't like the look of you at all. I can see

136

you are not looking after yourself. You are as thin as a rake.'

'I was never a fat man, Billy.'

We drank a pot of tea together, talking about the painting I had done on the table and he said he was going to see the Pension Officer, see if he couldn't get me extra money.

When that Pension Officer did come, he did sneak a look round the walls, but only once. Seeing the paintings made him sniff. 'Your nephew William Wallis brought it to our attention that your pension might not be adequate to your needs.' He took the top off a fountain pen. 'I've come to ask you a few questions about those.'

I said I had a landlord now. I did own the house at one time, having brought it from Daniel Hollow for ninety-three pounds. Mr Armour had settled with Mr Spink to buy the house for fifty pounds. I had lived on that for a while. Spink now says he might sell the place on to Mr Care on the understanding that Mr Care is not to let it go until I am dead. So I go on paying him a few shillings rent. What I been doing since I spent that fifty pounds was to sell one or two bits and pieces. I said nothing about selling paintings, of course.

I said I did not need much. I got by on two penny-ha'penny bread loaves a week. I spent four shillings a week at Mr Baughan's shop and would get myself half an ounce of tobacco twist. 'I chew the stuff – I got into that habit at sea, when I had no time to smoke. I get heartburn these days when I feel I have to do it, though.'

I did notice the other day my shirt cuffs were grimy and when I took it off the collar was dirty too. I couldn't stand to look down at my fallen chest, the muscles withering on my arms. I am so lost in painting I don't bother with anything else.

What was nasty about losing your teeth is that food falls out your mouth and stains your guernsey. That is not nice at all if you do not wash it every other day. I try to keep up with my underwear when the weather allows it. There's a basket of washing I got waiting to hang up. I had to fit it all in somehow.

'We learn to know our place, Mr Wallis.' He was writing, whether it was what I was saying, I don't know. 'As you get older, you must feel your infirmity the more,' he said.

'No,' I said. 'All it means is that everything takes that much more of an effort.'

In the end, I said I had had it all, anyway. I would never mind what he decided, one way or the other. 'I swam against the tide all my life; too late to do it any different now,' I said.

The Pensions Officer was a man given to sigh a great deal. The whole of his life was tiring him out. He was putting on his bicycle-clips when Sarah Rainford came by with her shopping basket to give him the fruit of her wisdom. 'To be kind, we say that Mr Wallis is what we Cornish call pixielated,' she said. 'Not everybody can become a fully paid-up member in St Ives, no matter how long they live here. Mr Wallis's case is doubly hard; he is a man who knows his own mind, and is sure where he is going. He is never easy to come at at the best of times. Who knows what goes through his head? His tongue grows sharper the older he gets.'

Soon as they had gone, Susan was there in the corner,

saying: 'Look at you! Don't you know you got fleas? Don't you know you are starting to stink?'

That is what they were too polite to say about me. Well, she had never been afraid to tell the truth, and I was getting near the end of my rope. 'You know nothing, Alfred; you never did know much, except about ships and the sea, which is no use at all on land. You are the talk of the road, I hope you know.'

I said, I told her, 'You get hold of something, you never let go!'

'We all make our own cross, Alfred, and you have no one else to blame. Mr Holley was right. You got no moral fibre, Alfred.'

In the end, I threw a blanket over the table and got under it.

I know Hitler is another name for Satan. Satan has got out of my bedroom now and is everywhere in the world. He is sinking ships, drowning sailors every night, every day, God rest their souls.

I got the biscuit tin down. Soon as I took off the lid, the smell of old crumbs in a damp corner sent me back. The biscuit box at sea had to last the voyage; those biscuits were hard to chew but tasty the first weeks. After that, you could never know what might come out of a biscuit, so you had to knock it about a bit. You got anything from a grub to a moth, or a nest of weevils. They used to put bone dust in with the flour to harden in the baking, and it was that the insects liked to breed in.

Some days, I can't abide a certain place; the air there is ice-cold. I get out of it quick and sit near the fire. Another time, that cold won't be there, or I find it in another spot. Queer that. One night, on a sudden, the glass on her picture cracked across. Cost me a shilling to get it fixed.

★

I told her that a barracuda is so fast that you don't see it coming until it's too late. It keeps a larder of every sort of fish to hand. They all swim in a bunch, afraid to break away. Not even when the barracuda comes in to have his tea. They seem to share each other's fear, and I've seen a fifty and more together that way. You got no chance yourself if you fall in the sea anywhere near a barracuda.

I had seen Alethea Garstin sitting on the sand by the harbour, near where I had my store. She said she was writing a letter about lizards and violets – oh, and primroses and white Godrevy. Everything in St Ives was so beautiful.

'You don't look too happy, I can tell,' she said.

'I'm in a fix here,' I said, not wanting to say I was missing the store, my pony and cart. 'I got some paintings I want to send off to Mr Ede. I need help to tie them, post them off.'

'Don't fret at all, Mr Wallis,' she said. 'I'll come up and help you do that.'

She was true to her word. She came the next morning to wrap and tie up those pictures.

'Alethea is a name I like,' I said. 'It's a good name for a ship.'

'Better than Garstin,' she said.

'My mother was called Jane Ellis, and she was from the Scilly Isles,' I said. 'If I half close my eyes at sunset, I see her well enough to talk to her.'

'That's a fine old Cornish range you have there,' she said.

'Susan kept it cleaner than I do,' I said, 'buffing away at the black lead until it shone. I give it a wipe-over when my spit misses the grate.'

I asked if she knew Mr Ede. When I did not hear what she said, I asked if he was an artist.

'No. He is with the Tate Gallery in London. He can do a lot for you, Mr Wallis. They have taken you up.'

'That's what the police do.'

Alethea laughed.

'I was never an artist,' I said. 'Nobody taught me. I made myself one. I am a child of change; I can only say that's always been my secret. Even now, in these hard times, I get by. Just as, if I don't have ivory or horn, I go along the beach and find a bone bleaching: that will make a good stock for a knife. I can handle any tool, auger, axe or adze, drawknife and spokeshave. I can weave withies into a lobster-pot.'

I smiled over the way she was trying to tie the parcel up. People will only stand idle to watch a greenhorn mend a net if he's all fingers and thumbs. Once he gets the knack they don't bother.

'What you need there is a firm sailor's knot,' I said, showing her. Then I picked up a rope I found on Porthmeor. I had it drying in the hearth. 'Say you have two ropes that are not the same thickness. First you will make a bend, the bowline is best. You can make it easy and quick by closing a loop in the thicker rope and then set four or five racking turns in it with the thinner rope, until you tuck the end under in a last racking turn, see.'

Her eyes blinked once or twice.

When I woke up, I did not know whether it was the wind or the voices until I could make out the words. I thought somebody was at the door, and went to answer. Soon as I did, a stone came over my shoulder, and very near to knocking my eye out. The other went over my head. I shut the door quick and shot the bolt. The children must have carried those stones off the beach. One had hit the wall by Susan's picture.

'Steer clear. This means you.' – I wrote on a piece of card I put in the window.

A man is not safe on his own doorstep, these days. There's a lot to be said for peace of mind. I used to have it, but not now, not any more. You have to lock your house up, or you never know who might get in.

Going down the Digey, I thought the boy running had a bundle of my paintings under his arm. I shouted for him to stop, then broke into a trot. But by the time I got to the corner he had gone. I kept my eyes open, going down the hill, in case he was set to jump out from some court when I least expected it. When he did not, I felt the cold settle in my bones. Jog jog jogging down the Digey, with the harbour below, so that you see more the nearer you get.

I was safe in Mr Curnow's barbershop in Gabriel Street. I look up and there's the photograph taken in 1894, when the river was in spate and flooded families out in the Stennack, knocking holes in their walls. There is another picture of Mr Bohenna when he was in his prime. Where you'll find him now is dead in Madron.

'They tell me a stone of haddock will fetch seven shillings now,' said Mr Keach. 'You would be glad to get three shillings not long ago. No doubt the war has done that. It was the same last time.'

Close your eyes and you can just drift along on that talk.

'You remember Mr Tregurtha. He used to bring a stool out and sit in the sun with his glass. He played the fiddle all night long.'

'The town has to live and work to the tides; you got no way round that.'

'Spurdogs by the dozen thrashing, eager to get among shoals of herring and pilchards and rip your nets apart. It was always rough weather then.'

I said, 'We used to have two things to help us get through rough weather. You would slit a hole in a canvas bag of oil, colza was best, so that it drained out slow to smooth the sea around the ship, or you could tow a couple of long ropes astern that would help keep her bow up.'

When is the day of the Annual Show? Well, it was then, they said, when they came, when artists all over town opened their doors to the public. Mr Ben and Miss Barbara brought along a Miss Gardner. She could not get over that I had never in all my life used a telephone. She was talking about the gasworks being a blotch on the beauty of Porthmeor. I said there was a gasometer up there blotting the stars out when I got here, so I was used to it. The workers all had yellow faces; some nights you could smell it, too. 'I get my cinders there when I can't afford coal. I can remember the council getting into hot water tipping gaswork cinders on Porthmeor Beach. That was around the time it was in danger of falling down the cliff and they had to shore it up.'

There was some other young man with them. They said his name was Lanyon. He bought a picture of mine, and had to ask what the crew was doing. 'Mind your own business,' I told him. That shut him up for a while.

I had to tell him that a gaff was a spar to lengthen the top of a fore-and-aft sail that isn't set on stays. Not that he understood any of that, from the look in his eyes.

'All the boats in that fleet had a soul, a beautiful soul,

shaped like a fish: so the fish I've painted there aren't fish at all. What good would you be without a soul, eh?'

Mr Naum Gabo came later, alone. He said I knew his wife; she had bought some of my paintings. I knew he was a sculptor from Russia; a deep man who knew about physics, chemistry and engineering. I did not mind he did not have much to say; I can understand that better. He walked about, then asked if he could take one out into the road to see the colours. He did not say much, but I felt he was taking a good close look, sharp as a bird for what's going on. He was not talking to me, but I caught a few of the things he was saying. He said that to burn a ship was the easiest way to get at the copper on her bottom, and they did a lot of that after the Great War. Who got the first cargo of tea from China home made the most money, he said, but, after they dug the Suez Canal, sail was fighting a losing battle against the trade that used it. Those ships may have been beauties to look at, and they were certainly workhorses that carried every size and sort of cargo. They kept the wheels of industry turning, but it took too many men to handle them and keep them afloat. If they had not had reliable pumps, they would have sunk. Even in port, somebody had to work to keep them afloat. That was very true.

When he left, I wrote 'Alfred Wallis Studio' on a piece of card and stood it on the doorstep. Nobody came in after that. I was taking it in, late afternoon, when Mrs Peters came out to go down the shop before it closed.

'You're getting a many callers today, Mr Wallis,' she said.

I gave a nod. 'So I am; it's been opening day – all the studios in St Ives have had people looking in.'

'Is that a fact, now?'

Mr Adrian and his wife were in before I could bolt the door, and I slammed the Bible shut to show I did not like that. They should have known I cover my painting with newspapers on a Sunday and read nothing but the Bible. I said the only reason I would let them see anything was because I was too old and too ill now to look after myself, and I did not plan to paint any more. Mr Adrian said he was sorry to hear that, but I knew my own mind. I said it did not have anything to do with knowing my own mind. 'I'm too old. I can't see the sense in it any more,' I said. 'I'm sick. It's time I was off to the workhouse, because that's the only place I got left to go. Nobody is going to look after me, for sure.'

'What does Mrs Peters say?'

'Why don't you ask her? She has enough to do, and my tongue would turn rusty in my throat before I'd say a word of it to her. She doesn't want to hear about how bad I feel.'

He said he would have a word with her before he left. Had I had a visit yet from Sven Berlin?

'Who?'

'He is a young sculptor who came to live in St Ives recently. I showed him your work and told him about you. He says he will come over to see you. He wants to buy one of your pictures.'

'He better come quick, is all I can say, or he'll find an empty house!'

If Mr Adrian has a fault, it is that he will launch into a painting, talking about it as if I was not there. He makes it sound as if I had nothing to do with it, as if someone else had done it. This time it was about a painting I had done of Saltash, and he had to take care with it because the paint was still wet.

'What does it remind you of, Margaret?' he said. 'Look at those planes leading down to the bridge.'

She shook her head, giving up.

'It's a Cubist picture,' he said.

No mention was made of the ship anchored at the bottom of the road, or that I was a child looking up at high buildings when I saw it.

Mr Adrian was a busy man; he can never stay long. He says he has a market garden to run, as well as all the writing he does. I could tell, though, that Mrs Margaret felt sad about going.

I lean down to the fire with a paper spill and light my pipe. Am I talking to myself too much, Mother? It is you I'm talking to, isn't it? The flame steadies in the glass, a coal hums in the grate. I got the oil-lamp but what was snug has become a terrible place, Mother. You know what I mean?

It has got so that I do not trust myself to open my razor to shave. Who do I expect to see in the glass? It was so bad I had to break the damn thing; then I couldn't see myself anyway. There is one looking-glass for saints to see themselves in, and another for sinners; there is quite another for a man who does not want to see where he has been over his shoulder. Like the blind man, I can smell the goatskins, and I am alone on the island. When I can stand no more I go out in the dark. Anywhere is better than the house.

I went down to Porthmeor. Not a light was showing anywhere, nor out to sea. I gave myself up to the sharp rain; nobody heard my voice in the roar I knew of the waves.

At daybreak I awoke curled up under a boat. It was still

raining; I could feel it striking. Somebody walked by; I saw his boots. I felt a fool under there, so I did not move. He came back, slower then, and I guessed he was a fisherman gone by. When I got out from under, there was nobody to see on the beach. There was that light that tells you the sand still holds water. Never mind it was grey, and that the wind whined and hummed, I could see a pale sun behind rain-clouds. There was no sign it would let up. Shivering, I went down by the edge of the sea to walk.

I shake my head soon as I hear the hoofbeats come up fast behind. I have to turn, though, and when I do I see a big black horse come thundering through the sea. Colonel Benson's girl is riding it; every button is undone, and her big breasts billow side to side out of her wet silk shirt. She flies by, and so close I hear the horse's breath roar in my ear; all the sand it kicks up stings my face.

I must have given a shout, for she reined about and came on to run me down again. If I had not got out of the way, I would have been knocked to death by those hooves. I set off to run to get off the beach. I don't think I ran so fast in my life. Soon as I got to the steps, I had to look back. I kept looking to make sure it was true, but by then they were a blur in the sea mist, and I knew I could never be sure.

Getting inside the cottage, I fell asleep by the fire in wet clothes. I had done that often, but when I woke I could hardly lift my arms. I felt so poorly I got my clothes off and got into my box.

Mr Armour and Mr Edwards came knocking to find out how I was doing. I had turned in early; I could not find the strength to raise my head out of my box.

They had missed me coming round to pass the time of day, they said. I could see by their faces that they had given me up for dead. Mr Edwards stayed with me, sitting beside the couch, his long white fingers holding on to my box, while Mr Armour went to phone the doctor.

It came as a shock to see that my face was black when he held a mirror to my lips. He soon got my shirt open to listen to my chest, and I heard him say I had bronchitis.

Seems to me I've had more than a touch of that lately.

Any man who goes over the side in a rough sea has no chance; so much is happening it would be cruel to throw a lifesaver and prolong his agony. He knows he is swept away. Who would want to be a captain then? He sat at the right hand of God and had His ear on who should live or die.

I did not go out much at all last winter, at best a few steps to the corner; people brought the few things I needed. Now I feel it coming on again.

'What do you think it is, Mr Wallis?'

'My lungs are set to burst I live so long under water.'

'From the sounds of that cough, you got bronchitis again.'

I sat by the fire. I could see Mrs Peters outside. When she looked my way, I could make out by her lips what she said. My door was open, and the Relieving Officer better go along with her. Mr Wallis was deaf; go in there alone, the old man would not understand a word you say. They knocked and came in, and Mrs Peters come over and asked was I going to Madron?

'I don't know about that,' I said.

The Relieving Man said they best leave it till morning. He was the sort of man you look over your shoulder and, if you see him shake his head, you are dead in a week. I was afraid, but I could not show it. I knew it was coming, Mother. You and I both knew.

Mrs Peters was not with him the next day. She stood with her arms folded, sometimes bending low to look in the window. What she does is cup her hands around her face like this, against the light on the glass. I did not want to hear what he said, kept on nodding enough to send him away. He went out and I saw him say that it was all right, 'Mr Wallis has his mind made up. I'll bring the car at six to fetch him.' Mrs Peters looked in where I sat, shaking her head. After he went, she came back.

'I know damn well where I'm going,' I said. 'Madron Workhouse! That's where he's taking me.'

'Never you mind, my dear. Don't let your heart break about it, Mr Wallis.'

I wanted to cry, but held back. You cry when the wind's in your face, when you can't stop the tears. She stood by the door, going. 'I don't care no more where I go to be looked after,' I said.

I got ready after that. I warmed up some water and washed myself top to bottom. I had clean underwear; I took a handful of mothballs out of my Sunday-best suit and put it on. After I gave it a brush, I sat by the fire to wait.

When Mrs Peters knocked again, she said. 'You got your clean shoes on, Mr Wallis, but you forgot your socks.'

'Not going to do that – not till he *come* for me!'

Mrs Peters gave a nod. She knew I had my mind set. I gave her the twenty pounds I had saved; said, look after this, Mrs Peters, it's to pay for a proper grave in Barnoon when I go. She knew what I meant. I had said it enough times.

I shut my eyes.

A sail loft has a smell all its own: the tar, the beeswax to soften the twine for sewing the strips together. Look after a sail, and it will do you ten to fifteen years. I was there; I could smell it all until I heard the car, then I let Mrs Peters put my socks on. It was the last thing she could do for me, and she was motherly. 'I can't make my mind up about that Bible,' I said.

'Better not take it,' she said. It was big, too heavy to lumber up there.

'What I got is my magnifying glass, see to read the papers, and scissors to trim my nails,' I said.

I was nearly out the door when the Relieving Man looked back. 'You are going without your watch, Dad.'

Why do I need a watch? But I went and took it down from where I hung it by the mantelpiece. I did not look at Susan; I did not look at my father. I was going, and I knew I would not come back. I kept my eye on the sea as we drove up to Stennack, all along Porthmeor and out to Clodgy. Then, high on the moor, I had a last faint sight of the Island in the sunset.

I said I had to piss but it was more to feel the air and try to hear the birds that sing on the moor of an evening. I listened hard, but heard nothing.

It was near to where Mr Bohenna had asked me to stop the cart that day, when I was taking him at last to Madron. Mrs Bohenna had died, and he was left alone with nobody to care at all. He said unless I took him in my cart to Madron, he would not go else.

It had come on to rain. Mr Bohenna never minded that. What he had never wanted was to turn into one of those old salts that sat on the pier with nothing better to do than chop and snap at any thing that came their way. If they were not by St Leonard's Chapel, well out of the wind, you'd see them lined up outside the Shamrock Lodge.

'Do you remember those two elephants there once, walking around the harbour?' His smile was the first I had seen. 'That made their day. Everybody came running from far and wide to see.'

I could not say why a man was born to scour the sea in search of a livelihood.

No more could he.

'Just as we were thinking it was not worth getting the trawl wet, they were all about us,' Mr Bohenna said. 'Any fish with teeth will fight to the last; it will bite a hole in the net, if it can. You know pilchards do riddle, coming quick to the surface. I can hear that sound in this rain now, and that's all it is. When our net came up, the mesh was aflame with a blue-white light.'

As the car turned in the workhouse gate, I knew that from there, if I could make it out, was a view of Mount's Bay and clear over to the Lizard.

How long have I been here, Mother? I went to bed, now I am wide awake. I was low when I come here. I had given up for dead. At 59°N, there are strange latitudes around Cape Farewell. One day the sails are frozen stiff, the next it's so warm the crew will shed their shirts. All this changing and change about means that there are fogs, often black as night; the cold gets in the compass, so you don't know where you are.

Otherwise everything is regular here. Reminds me how it used to be aboard ship. Up at five-thirty in the morning the cook had coffee ready for the deck watch at four bells. Somebody gives the helmsman a spell so he can drink a cup.

At seven bells, the watch goes aft for breakfast: coffee, biscuits and margarine or marmalade. At eight bells they relieve the deck watch that comes in to eat theirs.

At seven bells on a Sunday night we got pea soup, rice or potatoes with salt beef or pork. The meat came out of a tin, done up into a stew.

What it seems, is that none of them knew I had been brought to Madron. It was Miss Alethea who had gone round Back Road, and Mrs Peters had told her they had taken me away. She came up to visit soon as she could. 'Why now, Mr Wallis,' she said, 'how are you then? Everybody was worried where you had got to.'

'Who was that, then?'

'Mr Leach said he knocked, and went off thinking you were out.'

'No, they got me with my guard down, that's all,' I said. 'You go through a bad patch and people get to thinking what's best.'

'Yes, they tend to do that.'

'How do they know?'

'They never do.'

'I lie here mostly looking at the wall,' I said. 'Seems that's the furthest I can see now: green, then a black line, then cream up to the ceiling somewhere up there – something like those colours I would use painting.'

She gave my hand a motherly pat.

'You tell Mr Ben I'm stuck here. Tell him I got to see him.'

The second time Mr Ben and Mr Adrian came up to study my misery, I was out of bed. They didn't get much change out of me when they first came. Soon as I saw Mr Ben come in, I said, 'I been wanting to see you.' I went over to him. 'Black, white and green. Enamel, in tins, sixpence each.'

He knew what I meant.

'No blue?'

'No, I want black, white and green.'

Those watercolours Mr Ben had brought – I said, how can I use those? All French to me, so I hid them in the corner there. I know I'm madder here than I was in Back Road. I told them, I wanted to get up out of bed, but the nurse says I can't, and will she let me have my baccy and pipe, damn her? I sent her to fetch the Master. 'Now, now, Mr Wallis,' says he, 'this will never do. We don't stand tantrums here, even if you are Michelangelo.' They all laugh at that. You tell that man, Mr Ben; you put him in his place! They treat me as if I was dogshit on their shoe. Unless you speak up for me, I don't know what will happen.

Mr Ben had to smile over how long my hair had grown. He said that Miss Alethea had told him I was a prophet in here. She seemed to think I had got the measure of all these old buggers. I said I had no interest at all in hearing what any of them had to say. If they gave ear to me it was because I had seen more than they had. You see a green crab run on a beach, it can go two feet a second if it wants. Down South, the long-legged red-and-yellow one runs ten feet a second. They scare the hell out of you. There were days not long ago I felt I could do that still, moving furniture for Mr Armour, or my trousers rolled up so my legs got the air as I walked. The thing about most crabs is that they live and die a few miles from where they were born.

A lot of people in there were like that. I got nothing to

say to most of them. All I know to talk about is the Bible, the sea and ships. What do they care about those? They will tell you any story, broadcast it, too, things they think you want to hear about – how they lost a shilling and found a farthing, or the other way round. What a man needs is more worship in the valleys and on the mountain-tops, I said.

They do not want a man to have memories, a man who can tell how things used to be. They say we have to live for today now, and not think on how it was. If you can let go in your mind, it all rolls back, sea upon sea, sleet into snow, aloft and on deck, the dolphins fleeting under the keel.

'They've driven half the old buggers mad in here. You look around before you go; it's a Punch-and-Judy show in some quarters.'

Often they say more by their silence, with how they turn away from you, not hearing a word you utter. All they do is listen to hear about the war here, and some will not do that. 'They say it's not a workhouse any more. They call it the Madron Public Assistance Institution, but I'm damned if it's not the same place.'

The Master came to have a word when they had gone. He was on about something they had shown him – my name in a magazine and I had paintings in the Museum of Modern Art in New York.

I sit out there some days; they got a sunny wall, and I can get in a corner and forget my troubles for an hour or so. They tell me you can see right across Mount's Bay from the drive – even if I could, I've had enough of that. I got a corner in that dresser there where I can keep my painting stuff, but I don't do much. I draw with crayons more than

154

anything, and that is not the same. If I'm going to paint at all, the weather has to be fine, so I can go out there and sit at the table in the sun. It's not often, though; I can't get in the mood.

They said that the Relieving Officer has got his hands on the twenty pounds I saved to get a proper burial, and he was set to burn all my pictures. So they went round to my cottage to fetch them out of there: Mr Ben, Mr Adrian and his wife. It was Mrs Margaret the fleas leaped on first; then they bit all of them. Mr Ben was quick; he knew what to do, never mind he was wearing his white suit and cap. He ran off to the sea, went out into it until it was over his head. Mr Adrian and his missus made haste to get home, left their clothes along with my paintings in their garage and ran naked for a bath. Now they got swarms of the buggers in the house that bite worse than I do. If I know fleas, they won't get rid of them in a hurry.

Mr Adrian and Mr Ben talk about getting my fleas out, and doing the cottage up, then find some woman to come in to look after me. Mrs Peters, I don't think! What they won't do, and it's the one thing I want, is come and get me out of this hole. I am at the mercy of the Master, who is in the hands of the Board of Guardians. We are paupers; that's what he calls us.

I am here going on fourteen months now, near as I can make out. I saw those rhododendrons bloom out there, so it was spring then. I believe nothing of what Mr Ben and Mr Adrian say about the war making it hard to find somebody to look after me.

Just a flurry of breeze blows in to lift the lace curtain. I can feel the heat on the wall, and the cobbles sizzle. If I were down there on the Wharf, I'd smell the tar come in waves off the keels of the boats, alive in the sun. To caulk a boat, you hammer a twist of tarry oakum into the groove – one line, then another; three in all – that done, you rub the pitch mop slow and easy along the side. The sun beats on your neck because a sunny day is the best time to do that job.

I think it might be worth my while to see Mr Leach. So I bundle a few paintings and take them along in case I can sell him one, without meaning to. I seen him work there before, and I like the way his foot sets the treadle going back and forth, not saying a lot as his hands shape the clay. He can do it so fast that bowls and pots come up like magic. You see him get the red-hot pot out of the furnace and put it in a bucket lined with newspapers. I always thought it a strange line for a judge's son. He told me he was born in Hong Kong. China always crops up; Mr Adrian's missus came from there, too.

Never mind these old buggers around, I don't; and all I got to say to these nurses is to mind what company they keep. Lately I've had that sail loft on my mind a lot. Up in there, now, there were webs hung everywhere, glinting silver in the sun. There were lobster-pots, wormy baskets, dusty beer bottles full of spiders and a matchbox chock-a-block with dead matches. You go up, you have to watch your step on those boards. They are so full of worm you could go straight through. You see only your footprints in the dust; but you have to call out a name or two before you set foot in there, just in case you see something, someone, you do not want to see. I never went there often then; nothing was what it was, and it hurt deep down, if I could admit it.

Mr Ben gave me four sketchbooks for Christmas and I had

got one of those pads out to do a drawing of Noah's Ark. I had done it before: the house on a ship that Noah and his family had, aground on top of Mount Ararat. We all hope to get a berth on that boat. Then the nurse came in and said a book writer, a Mr George Manning-Sanders, was there to see me.

I looked round the corner first, and I saw him by his car. I shook my head, saying I did not want to talk to him.

'He's driven all the way from St Ives,' the nurse said.

'Don't give a bugger about that!'

Just then, Mr Manning-Sanders turned and caught me there before I could get out of sight. He waved and came over smiling. I nipped back to pack up my pad and crayons, which I did just as he came in the courtyard.

'Mr Wallis?' he said, holding his hand out to shake. Call him George, he said.

I never met him before, but he talked as if I had always been his best friend or something very close. He wanted to know too much. He did not ask anything about painting; what he wanted was to know the far end of me. I got the feeling he had come to use me, but I could not think why anybody would do that. Any life I have had has been my own, and nobody else's business.

I wrote on a piece of paper that he better write down what he wanted.

It was easy then to make out I couldn't read a word.

Had he brought anything I could use to paint with, or paint on? Some bad cardboard I got had ridges in it. How was a man supposed to use that bloody stuff? As chance would have it, a fleck of spit flew out of my mouth and caught on his eyelash. It was as if I had stung him in the face on purpose. He wiped it fast as he could get his handkerchief out of his pocket. From that diabolical look of his, I saw then who Manning-Sanders was.

I was vexed, trying to get away then, backing into the room where all the others were sitting. He did not take the hint, and came on after. I could see it all, soon as it started, and those old buggers thought I couldn't, making out behind my back that I was touched, by screwing at their own empty heads. I threw the crayons and the pad across the floor and shouted, 'You lot siding with him against me? You don't know who you're dealing with! You got no idea! I shipped with men from every part of the world, but you old buggers take the biscuit. You don't have the sense you were born with. They can do what they like with you, and you would never know. You deserve all you get. Ask for more! Ask for more, why don't you?'

By then, I was swearing blue fire, and the nurses come running in to get a hold of my arms. Mr Manning-Sanders was picking up the stuff I threw on the floor while I shouted him to keep his black hands off it. If he had been sent for anything to do with that, I shouted, 'You tell Mr Ben I'm not waiting for Christmas for some proper paints!'

I was rigid, shaking; I pointed at him as he tried to get out the door with a lordly wave goodbye to all those buggers. 'You, you're as full of shit as they are. Get off back where you belong! Don't you bother coming here again. I got no time for you.'

You know I was a motherless child without schooling. Anything I know, I had to teach myself. When I was nine, I went as a cabin boy and cook aboard a schooner in the Bay of Biscay. All I knew was how to hoot like an owl, a trick I had taught myself. Long division was as much a mystery to me then as it is now.

I don't feel well. Is this the hour I draw my last breath?

Remember in Newlyn, I was mending nets and felt low, my throat sore, my nose runny? Old Grimes knew it was the venom left by dead jellyfish in the nets had got into my hands. It's in the nature of some things to be poisonous. Medusas he called them. He knew the Latin names, too. You see them here in summer, but he had seen jellyfish in the Arctic frozen solid in ice thaw out and drift on their way. Mr Grimes took a stake in undersea creatures after a scabbard-fish struck him off Madeira. He had a picture of every fish that swims in the sea. He would show his maimed hand, and was fond of telling how he came close to death.

There was a myriad Portuguese men-o'-war that summer, big and blue, under sail with their crests up. Some were seven feet across. Enough electric to power a wireless, Grimes would say, with a laugh. They live for the light – they die when they sink. There are poison fish at sea, as many as there are snakes on land, Mother. Some will kill you dead. There are father-lashers up near Greenland, all of five feet long, dark marks across yellow spine fins, with brown backs that go to a pale yellow under the belly, dappled so with spots you don't see them. They come at you with their gurnards' heads, with poison spines all along the gill-cover.

Remember those times I was sick aboard ship. Nothing is worse than to rock in the cradle of the deep with no mother to hear your cry. 'Thrice was I beaten with rods, once was I stoned, thrice I suffered shipwreck, a night and a day I have been in the deep.'

I woke up thinking I heard that old fishwife bawl

pilchards, the last I recall of her. One of these old biddies has a look of her now, but could never be as strong. She is out of an album now. She had a strap around her head that held the basket on her back; it would nip her hat-brim over her ears. So she's still here, and the other woman too. Listen to them talk, Mother, as I lie there on that table. They wash me and lay me out, your baby, Mother. 'Help me over with him, my dear,' says one old biddy. The other says, 'Why, he's no more than skin and bone.'

When they did get corpses ashore, they laid them on the beach; those with faces that were too bad they'd cover with a bit of sailcloth. One still had his watch in his waistcoat pocket, and an awful grin that a man felt he had to thumb out of his mouth. To make a clean breast of it, I don't look as broken as all that, what the sea has thrown up at last. I'm clean, but the minute they go, I see dust in the sunlight settle on my face. What skin the sun has not burnt is too milky and thin; you see the veins under it that kept my blood going night and day all those long years. I'm near forgetting who I was, long gone is any sign of that boy left in a wet fo'c'sle, afraid of the dark, of the sea.

Is that Alice Fincher I see there? No, all is lost now.

> *Her lips were red; her eyes were brown,*
>   Mark well what I do say,
> *And her hair was black and it hung right down,*
>   *I'll go no more aroving with you, fair maid.*

One year the *Coast of Bohemia* was there, all of us aboard, the next I could see no sign of her. I could never tell where she had gone. None of them were plain shipmates, but we got by together; I was happy until it was too late. Those were the days when I was nimble and sure-footed; I ran as fast as a monkey along a yard. Got her name out of Shakespeare, they say. Somebody had his tongue in his cheek – look for Bohemia on a map, and you'll see it is a hundred miles from the sea.

Don't they say that we are all in the same boat? What did any one of us know about the others except we heard it from someone else, or it would come up during a calm spell? Two died of the plague in Morocco. One of them was Peter Grunewald. He said he was born in Colmar; I found out later that he was from a Sussex seaside village. He turned up aboard as a stowaway, said he been round France and Spain on foot, staying in monasteries. He could drop a line over the side and haul up any fish you cared to name. His eyes were blue; he had a mandolin, and sang songs that broke your heart. The mate fetched up in Cuba; the bosun died in the Virgin Islands. One man could play any tune on his accordion, which he died doing in the streets of Paris. The carpenter, Ironfoot Jack, would drag his lame leg up and down the deck on an oval nine-inch stand. We had two drunken painters; when the one died, the other stumbled out of a bar and was run down by a horse. The last I see of them, I was riding on a tram by the sea. The rain came hard; the windows had fogged over. Their wigwam had blown away on the sands; soaked to the skin, they stood under the bare poles arguing on their wet bedding. They did not see me go. As a sailor, you learn never to go until they call your name.

It comes to this for us all; this is how I lost you, Mother.

I used to fear the day the sea shall give up its dead. I used to listen hard sometimes, thinking I could hear the voices of the drowned.

They sent my coffin down to Penzance in a van and put it on a train, same as I did for Father. I was going home, too.

The label on the handle said Parc Owles, Carbis Bay. Mr Adrian was going to get more than fleas.

He was at his wits' end; he had to haste to St Ives and run round the harbour to find where to put my body. Who would take it off his hands? He struck lucky meeting Sven Berlin, who was sad to hear I had gone. He had found out more about my life than Mr Adrian ever knew. He said I had been in the Salvation Army, and he was sure that they would take care of their own. If Mr Adrian gave him some money he would go along to Mr Anthony for some flowers. I liked the look of Mr Sven, with his beard. I could tell he is strong, I could tell; he has worked in fields, digging, and he has a build on him to knock the hell out of granite.

Why do I lie here at latitude 38°20'N, longitude 17°15'W? The wind is fair, yet the half-brig drifts under a jib and foresail. One staysail lies on the foredeck; the rest are neatly furled aloft. She is derelict, heading north-west by north. Going alongside, the mate of the *Dei Gratia* hails her. Is this death, a ship adrift, the crew all gone? Nights alone in Back Road West, when I was most inward, I'd fear to wake aboard her. I would pull up the bedclothes, but the fear would not go away that I was there, alone, adrift. Where did they all go? If they had to weather a storm, why is the captain's wife's sewing-machine oil not spilled? Her thimble waits on the shelf; it does not roll underfoot. All her hats, crinolines, shawl-pins are here; there is a fan, a doll and cotton-reels. A white hymn-sheet glares on her rosewood harmonium. The four bunks in the fo'c'sle are damp, but all is orderly: sea boots and oilskins ready – food, razors and soap. All is shipshape; they have left their pipes behind. What sailor will go anywhere without a smoke? One barrel of their cargo of crude liquor is open but, if any of them drank that, they would be blind or dead. Did those three feet of water in the hold alarm the captain? No, never. Two men could pump that out in no time.

They left no message. Fair weather or foul; if there is evil about out here, it is hard to prove. We hope, we pray, we can steer clear, but life is shipwreck in the end.

A baby cries. What sort of a mother would leave it to cry so? I don't need too much of that, if that's how it's going to be. There are too many weeping now, what with the bombs falling.

My head feels hot, Mother; turn the pillow. It was never easy for either of us. You and I came into this world to suffer; that is what they ordained. I went; I died without a sound, no one left to talk to.

Let the lighthouse light me home now.

Here I lie, under Mr Sven's flowers; the scent is so sweet I can't smell the sea come in to lift the boats in the harbour.

Lord, they did try me, but I hope they never found me wanting. Old Sun's wife was in to look, but she is dead herself. She stands quiet in the light of the street lamp, wiping her eye with the corner of her apron as if she had just had a good laugh. Just as I wonder who else will drop by I'd rather not see – there is Susan. I know the bag. It is the same one she took years ago to the butcher's in Fore Street. I'm glad when she gives my forehead a quick kiss. She has business elsewhere. I speak Mr Bohenna's name, and Mr Swail's, but can hear nothing. I whisper Kezia's name, too, at first light, but the seagulls yelp and keen so now I cannot hear her voice. Life comes back to the wharf again. She is in those noises, the long swell rising and riding along the wall under milky clouds.

See there, where they dig my hole. I am at low ebb. Bugger me, I knew I would end up with the paupers, as I feared.

I lie up here in Barnoon, waiting to see who will come to see me go. Mr Adrian comes along the path with his missus and says, 'This has got to stop; this place is not right for Mister Wallis; he will not rest here.'

God bless him, he paid an extra four pounds ten shillings to save me from there, and they had to come back another day to bury me.

I can hear the rain on the lid, and on the umbrellas as they come behind. I see Jacob near, the last of the Wards, and Susan's grandchildren too. I see Major Holley and the Salvation Army band, and Mr Adrian and his wife Margaret Mellis; Mr Bernard is with Miss Barbara. He is lucky to escape with his life: a German mine on a parachute came down near his pottery. It blew next door all to bits. They bomb here regular as clockwork now, it seems. They hit that old gasworks there, and that was close, so it's as just as well I got out when I did. They got the old folks sit at home now of an evening making camouflage nets.

I wish I knew who asked Mr Manning-Sanders; I would give him a piece of my mind, if I did.

I am alone. There are wreaths around me; I can do without the Wards'. There is one from Mrs Israels' husband: 'In homage to the artist on whom Nature has bestowed the rarest of gifts, not to know that he is one' was what he wrote. There is another from Sven Berlin and his wife.

A soft rain falls.

All in all, it's not a bad turn-out for an old rag-and-bone man. None of it would be so if Mr Armour did not say, 'I have faith in you, Alf.'

I feel sprightly again, not heavy, no bones, and no body. They say Miss Barbara would not carve a stone. Lately, Mr Adrian got Mr Bernard to make a picture with a lighthouse on sandy yellow tiles. I can't get over the old bugger saw fit to give me a stick, though; I got by without one of those, but, sure enough, he has me to the life all right, going up the steps into the lighthouse at last. All it says is: 'Alfred Wallis, Artist and Mariner: Into Thy Hands O Lord.'

The best thing the sea can do is to bring you home. Under that green light, there is a darkness so deep I can't bear to think on it. At last I face the answer that has been waiting, long before I asked the question; do I drift aboard that derelict, or am I here, high up, where if the weather clears I'll be able to see out across Porthmeor?